FORGOTTEN DREAMS
A CHRISTMAS IN NEW ENGLAND STORY

KARI LEMOR

RYCON PRESS

FORGOTTEN DREAMS © 2020 by Kari Lemor

Cover Art by: Karasel

First Electronic Edition: October 2020

ISBN - 978-1-7348335- 4-6

First Print Edition: October 2020

ISBN - 978-1-7348335- 5-3

All rights reserved under the International and Pan-American Copyright Conventions. No part of this book may be reproduced or transmitted in any form or by any means, electronic or mechanical, including photocopying, recording, or by any information storage and retrieval system, without permission in writing from the publisher.

This is a work of fiction. Names, places, characters and incidents are either the product of the author's imagination or are used fictitiously, and any resemblance to any actual persons, living or dead, organizations, events or locales is entirely coincidental.

OTHER BOOKS BY KARI LEMOR

Storms of New England series - small town contemporary

1. Elusive Dreams - Erik and Tessa
2. True Dreams - Sara and TJ
3. Stolen Dreams - Alex and Gina
4. Broken Dreams - Nathaniel and Darcy

Special Storms of New England Books

Forgotten Dreams: A Christmas in New England story

Coming in 2021

5. Lost Dreams - Greg and Alandra
6. Faded Dreams - Luke and Ellie

Also coming in 2021

Love on the Line - romantic suspense series

1. Wild Card Undercover (rerelease)
2. Running Target (rerelease)
3. Fatal Evidence (rerelease)
4. Hidden Betrayal (new)
5. Death Race (new)
6. Tactical Revenge (new)

To Kristan, who inspires me to do great things and write better words.

I couldn't do this without you!

ACKNOWLEDGMENTS

So many people have given me support and encouragement on my writing journey. I wouldn't be here today if not for them. My husband who never even blinked when I wanted to retire from teaching to write full time. My children who are my biggest supporters and cheerleaders. Sagey who waved her purple pom poms furiously until I put more words on the page. And especially to my amazing TEAM, Meredith, Emily, and Kristan, who are always there helping me with any writing problem I have. You make me who I am!

And to all the beautiful winters spent in New England, you are the dreams of Christmas!

CHAPTER ONE

"What do you mean Janet and Joan can't come in today? It's the week before Christmas, and we've got a full house."

Kristan Donahue let out a deep sigh and tucked her long red hair behind her ears. She should have put it in her typical bun this morning, but with the chilly air outside, she'd wanted it down to keep her warm.

Macy Wagner, the office manager and bookkeeper for The Inn at the Falls gave a dainty shrug. "They called in sick. Said they have the flu. They both sounded pretty yucky."

"Why did they call you instead of me? They know I'm always here early."

Macy's impish grin appeared. "I'm sure they wanted to avoid the grand inquisition."

Kristan narrowed her eyes at their office manager. Macy had been a good friend for years and was one of the only people who could get away with saying something like that to her. Most of the other staff were terrified of her strict business persona.

"Do we know they have the flu or do they just want some

time off? We're booked solid the next few weeks, plus the Storm anniversary party next weekend." Janet and Joan were twins in their fifties who'd never been married. They were excellent workers…when they showed up. Usually, at least one of them came in while the other took a day off, but both of them? It couldn't have come at a worse time.

"I'm sorry. Don't shoot the messenger. If you're really stuck, give a yell, but I've got payroll to do today, so I don't have tons of extra time." With a whoosh of wild blonde curls, Macy did an about face and sashayed back to her office.

Just what she needed right now was to be shorthanded. Her family had owned The Inn at the Falls in Squamscott Falls, New Hampshire for over a hundred years. Last year, her father had decided to slow down his involvement and she'd been named manager. Her brother, Zachary, was more interested in the lifestyle of aquatic creatures than the comforts of humans here at the inn. Besides, with her degree in business, it was only logical.

The phone rang. She glanced around expecting someone else to answer it, except Joan was usually at the front desk. Grabbing the handset, she put on her gracious hostess voice, even if she felt like screaming.

"Good morning. Inn at the Falls. This is Kristan. How may I help you?"

She sat in the chair and opened up the registration menu on the computer. No, they didn't have any rooms currently, but yes, she could put them on a waiting list for New Year's Eve if someone canceled. As she typed, the bell over the door tinkled, and someone approached the desk.

Eyes never leaving the screen, she covered the receiver and whispered, "I'll be right with you."

A deep voice replied, "No problem."

The sound of it caused shivers to rush through her body. When she looked up, she froze.

Mark Campbell stood tall and erect, smiling at her with that stupid crooked grin that always made her knees weak. His dark hair was shorter in a military cut, and he filled out his BDUs with a body much more buff than when he'd left ten years ago. He was still so incredibly good looking it made her want to cry.

A voice on the other end of the phone brought her back to the present. "Yes, I've got your information. We'll be sure to call if we have any cancellations."

Standing, she brushed her hands down her skirt and tugged on the bottom of her cropped matching jacket. "Mark, hi. When did you get back in town?"

"Hey, Krissy." He was the only one who ever got away with calling her that. It had been ten years since she'd heard it. "Just got in a few minutes ago."

"Great. Here for Christmas?" And his first stop was to see her? What did that mean?

"Yeah, visiting the family. But Edele has four kids, so I thought it might be better to get a room here."

So, she wasn't first on his mind. Of course, she wasn't. What an egotistical thing to think. He obviously hadn't thought about her in ten years. Unlike herself, who'd thought of him every day since he'd left.

"Oh, we're all booked up, I'm afraid." Could she offer him a place to stay at her house? She had an extra bedroom. She'd been good friends with his sister, Edele, for years, so it was only the neighborly thing to do. Right?

That crooked smile again. Darn, it hit her right in the heart.

"I've got a reservation."

Narrowing her eyes, she peered down at the computer and tapped a few keys.

"Oh, you do. Look at that." How had she missed Mark's name on the registration? This was just what she needed.

Her old boyfriend making her off kilter when she had to be at her best. Needed to prove to her father that he'd done the right thing making her manager. Shaking her head, she took a deep breath and tried to concentrate on her job. Which wasn't front desk clerk.

"Um, you're early. Check in isn't until three." She peeked at her watch. Barely ten.

"I did request early check in."

Another glance confirmed this. "Of course, you did. I'm afraid your room isn't quite ready yet. Check out isn't until eleven, and the guests are still in it. We'll need to turn over the room as well. Unfortunately for you, we're completely booked, so I don't even have another room I can put you in."

"I don't mind waiting. Can I sit here in the lobby?"

"It could be a few hours before the room's clean."

"I don't mind. I've got some work to do and the view here is pretty nice." His eyes focused on her. Yeah, don't fall for that again. He didn't mean the view of her. He must be talking about the gazebo on the town square across the street. It was beautifully decorated for Christmas.

She pointed to the room through the double doors to the right. "Feel free to grab a cup of coffee and some pastry in the breakfast room. It should be clearing out soon, and you can do your work in there if you want."

Picking up his duffel bag, he winked. "Thanks. Give me a yell when I can check in."

Kristan watched as Mark walked away. Holy Moly. Ten years had been very good to him. The twenty-year-old boy who'd broken her heart by enlisting in the navy and leaving her behind was replaced by a man who got that heart pumping back up to speed simply by smiling at her.

She was in trouble.

MARK SETTLED into a chair by the window in the breakfast room, making sure he still had a view of Kristan at the front desk. Man, how could she be even more beautiful than she'd been ten years ago? Her long, gorgeous red hair flowed down her back. He'd loved running his fingers through it. Especially when he kissed her.

After pulling his laptop from his bag, he started it up and logged in. He didn't have that much work to do, but he hadn't wanted Kristan to feel bad about the room not being ready. It was a good thing the inn was full. It meant business was booming.

A few people popped in and out of the lobby, and Kristan dealt with them politely and efficiently, her smile wide and genuine. When she scurried into the breakfast room for a cup of coffee, she glanced over and waved.

"Did you get enough to eat?"

Pointing to the plate that held his pastry, he nodded. "I'm good. Don't even worry about me."

She held the coffee cup in one hand and pressed her hand over her stomach with the other, then sighed. "It's really good to see you again, Mark."

"You, too. Maybe we could catch up at some point while I'm in town."

Her gorgeous green eyes widened. "That would be nice. I'd better get back. We're down two staff members today. I'm not usually on the front desk."

"Bet you're running the whole place." She'd always been exceptionally intelligent and put together.

She took a step closer, and her fragrance overwhelmed him with memories. Still a light floral scent that fit perfectly with her personality. "Actually, yes. I'm the manager here."

Why he did it, he didn't know, but he reached out, took her hand, and squeezed. "I never doubted you'd do great things."

She rolled her eyes, then glanced at their hands. "It's only a small family-owned inn. Hardly a career success."

He squeezed one more time, then dropped her hand. "Yet the reviews on this place are outstanding, and reservations are booked months in advance. That shows it's been well run. Congratulations."

The bell tinkled in the lobby, and she jerked her head to look who came in. "I've got to go. The guests in your room checked out a few minutes ago, and I sent someone to turn it over. It shouldn't be more than a half hour depending on how they left it."

"No rush. Thanks, Krissy."

Her cheeks flushed, then she clicked across the wood floor on her sensible heels. She'd always dressed so classically, even on casual dates. He'd liked that she took time with her appearance and always wanted to look good. Especially when she'd been on his arm.

Memories floated through his mind of all the time they'd spent together in the past. They'd started dating when she was sixteen and he was eighteen and had only stopped when he'd shipped off to the navy after finishing his degree in community college two years later.

God, he'd missed her. It had been ten years, but his heart still beat faster any time he got a glimpse of her rushing through the lobby. This reaction wasn't what he'd expected, but he shouldn't be surprised with how often he'd thought of her during his time in the navy. Just seeing her now, bent over a coffee table straightening some magazine, had his stomach doing flips and tying in knots. His military training was the only thing keeping him in his seat, instead of taking her in his arms and kissing her like he wanted to. Like he'd dreamed of so many times.

Edele hadn't mentioned Kristan ever getting married, but that didn't mean anything. His sister didn't know how often he'd thought of his old girlfriend and wouldn't have considered mentioning it.

Ten years was a long time. The only other time he'd seen Krissy was when his parents had died about five years ago. She'd been at the funeral but had stood way in the back. He thought she'd been dating Alex Storm at the time, but they hadn't come to the wake together.

He'd wanted desperately to go to her and have her hold him and make him feel better the way she always had in the past. But Edele and her kids had been devastated by the accident, and he'd needed to be stoic and brave for them. Luckily, Edele's husband, Jay, was a great guy, so Mark didn't have to worry about leaving his sister without someone to take care of her once he was back on board his ship.

But a funeral hadn't been the place to reacquaint himself with his old flame. Not only was she dating someone at the time, but he also still had time to serve for his country.

His computer screen showed confirmation that the navy had received his discharge papers, so that wasn't the case anymore. He studied the beautiful woman who stirred him even more than the girl ever had and wondered if it was too late.

A teenager in a white uniform scurried to the front desk and leaned in to talk to Kristan. Mark wished he could be that close to her. He'd gotten a whiff of her clean, floral scent earlier. It had brought him back to happier days, when the biggest dilemma was where to go on their next date.

The click of her shoes echoed on the wooden floor, and he tipped his chin up as she approached.

"Hey, Mark, your room is ready. Sorry for the wait." Her anxious face made him want to make everything perfect for her. All the time.

Standing, he said, "I'm the one who should apologize for getting here way too early. I could have stopped at Edele's first, but she and Jay are at work and the kids are all in school. This was a much nicer distraction."

Pink colored her cheeks as she handed over his key. "Let me know if there's anything you need."

Their hands touched as he took the key, and the old feeling of excitement and longing surged through him. But they weren't dating now. For all he knew she could be married or ready to marry another guy any day now.

"Thanks, Krissy. Appreciate it." He hefted his duffel bag over his shoulder and gave her the grin that used to make her giggle. Her eyes brightened, but she merely nodded and headed back to the front desk.

As he pushed in the chair he'd been using, fat snowflakes fluttering down outside the window caught his attention. They decorated the gazebo across the street with a blanket of white. One week until Christmas. Would the snow last until then? He'd been in a number of places at Christmas that had been too warm for snow, so he hoped this storm brought enough to last until he left again. The question was *where would he go?*

CHAPTER TWO

Mark slipped the key card into his pocket and headed down the hall of the inn. Hopefully, Kristan would be at the front desk again. Could he ask her to join him for a cup of coffee and one of the breakfast items in the dining room? He'd like nothing better than to see her and talk to her again.

After settling in his room yesterday, he'd taken a small walk around the downtown streets of Squamscott Falls. The softly falling snow had been magical. He'd then gone to his sister's house and had dinner with her, Jay, and the kids. It was great seeing his niece and nephews again, but they certainly had an abundance of energy. Ranging from four to ten, they put his sister through her paces. And had insisted Uncle Mark stay to put them to bed. There was no way he could refuse them.

But when he'd gotten back to the inn, Kristan was nowhere to be seen. Which was ridiculous that he'd even thought she would be. Even as manager, he didn't expect she'd put in thirteen-hour days.

Down the last few steps and he came out into the lobby.

The woman behind the front desk was attractive with curly blonde hair. But it wasn't Krissy, so he didn't spare her more than a cursory glance and nod.

Guess it was a solo breakfast today. He should enjoy it, since he'd spent the last ten years on board a ship eating in a cramped mess hall, shoulder to shoulder with all the other sailors.

Last night, he'd tried to get information out of Edele about Krissy's marital status, but each time he'd started the conversation, one of the kids interrupted and brought the topic back to them.

The front door opened as he crossed the lobby, and his heart jumped hoping it was Kristan. Alex Storm stood in the doorway, wiping his feet on the mat. He smiled when Alex looked up.

"Mark, how've you been? Still in the navy?"

Mark shook the man's hand. No need to be unfriendly, even if Alex had dated the woman who held his heart. Alex had dated his sister, too, and had been an absolute gentleman when they were together. Mark had made the decision to leave. It was his own damn fault Krissy had moved on to other guys.

"Still in the navy at the moment." Which was the truth, though not for much longer. But until he figured out what he wanted to do with his life, he'd keep that to himself. "What are you doing here? Did you move out of town and are back for the holiday?"

Alex looked surprised. "No, I'm still in town. Bought my parents' house, actually. We're having our wedding reception here in the summer, so we need to go over some of the details."

"Getting married, huh? Congratulations." Did he dare ask...?

"Yeah, I'm just waiting for Kristan, so we can start."

That answered his question. And sliced a hole in his gut. He managed to mumble something about good luck and waved as he trudged into the breakfast room.

After grabbing some coffee, a cinnamon roll, and a banana, he sat at the same table he had yesterday. One with a perfect view of the lobby and front desk. Why he didn't know. The last thing he needed was seeing his old flame with her new one.

When Kristan walked into the lobby, Alex's eyes widened, then he pulled Krissy into a hug with a peck on the cheek. Alex wasn't one for public displays of affection. Thank the Lord for small favors.

Sipping his coffee, Mark tried to pry his eyes from the sight. A woman with dark, wavy hair wearing a short, brightly colored skirt and thigh high boots bounced between Alex and Kristan. Whoa. She wrapped her arms around Alex's neck and planted a passionate kiss on his lips. Mark could feel the heat from here. But who—?

Kristan waved her hand out and followed the couple into a room on the other side of the lobby. Large glass windows showed the couple on a couch, the woman practically draped over Alex, whose face was a deep shade of pink. Kristan sat in a chair across from them and picked up a huge binder.

So Alex was marrying this other woman. Mark's shoulders released and his breath whooshed out of his body at the relief. He never pictured Alex Storm with someone like his fiancée, but he was glad it wasn't his Krissy. *His* Krissy. He had no right to call her that anymore.

He kept glancing across the lobby to where Kristan sat scribbling notes with the happy couple. Envy reared its head, but not for Alex being with Kristan. That he'd found love and someone to share his life with. Mark had wanted that, too. But he'd wanted more than a local education, and he hadn't wanted his parents to be burdened with that expense. Joining the navy had been the way to get it. Plus, the selfish part of him had wanted to see the world. Escape this little town and see what was out there.

And he had. He couldn't regret all he'd learned and seen in the last ten years. But studying the beautiful redhead across the way, he did have regrets. And they all centered around Krissy.

∼

"Here's a list of florists that we've used in the past." Kristan handed the printout to Alex and Gina. "Feel free to choose another if you've already got someone in mind."

Gina made a face at her fiancé. "Believe it or not, Alex hasn't gotten that far in planning the wedding even though it's only six months away."

Alex's mouth tightened, yet his eyes were soft as he gazed at the woman he loved. Kristan was thrilled that her old friend had finally found someone who loved him regardless of his super structured ways.

Her own gaze strayed to the breakfast room where Mark sat nibbling on a cinnamon roll. She'd been attempting to stay on task with the wedding couple, but her old flame, Mark, not Alex, kept distracting her. When she'd first seen Alex and given him a kiss, Mark had clearly scowled, but he seemed fine now. Did he not like Alex Storm? Everyone liked Alex. He was a super nice guy. Granted, a stickler for things like she was, but she'd never felt much beyond friendship with him, even though they'd dated for six months.

The reason for that was sitting staring at her now. Mark. He'd been the one on her mind every time she'd kissed Alex. It hadn't been fair to keep him hanging on when she couldn't get the memories she'd had with Mark to disappear.

Alex had found a woman as opposite from him as could

be, yet for some reason they worked. Gina challenged Alex's structured lifestyle and helped him loosen up.

Mark used to do that with her. He'd urged her to take risks and stop being so serious all the time. He'd made it easy for her to have fun and be silly. But with barely a word or discussion, he'd signed up for the navy and left town. Taking her heart with it.

Shaking her head, she examined her binder again. *Get your head in the game. Stop mooning over the man who didn't give you a second thought for ten years.* Yet she still couldn't pull her eyes away from him.

"We're still working on the guest list, so we'll get you an approximate head count as soon as we can." Gina's bubbly personality was infectious.

Kristan ran her finger down the page in front of her. "I've got all of the information I need at this point. In a few months, you can choose the dinner menu and decide on cake and decorations, but we don't need all those details yet."

Alex shuffled through the brochures on the coffee table between them and held up one for a local bakery, Sweet Dreams. "My Aunt Luci works here. She'll be making the cake for us, and my cousin, Sofie, will be doing the decorations."

Sofia Storm contracted many of the events at the inn. With her degree in Interior Design, she always made everything look stunning. Kristan had even hired her to decorate other parts of the inn. She'd done the entire lobby for Christmas.

"Yes, Sofie already gave me the plans for your grandparents' anniversary party next week. The menu is set, and your mother just called with the final count for dinner."

"Molly's so good at that list thing," Gina said getting to her feet.

Alex followed suit and held out his hand. "Thanks for your help, Kristan. We'll be in touch."

As Alex headed toward the door, Gina bounced over and enveloped her in a big hug. "You've been so great. I'm not even jealous of you anymore. Especially since that guy in the dining room can't keep his eyes off you. Go for it."

After Gina flounced toward Alex and they left, Kristan got the courage to check where Mark was. Yup, still staring at her, that crooked grin sending critters through her stomach. She was a big girl. She could handle it. She needed to ensure the dining room was stocked with adequate supplies, anyway.

"Did you have enough to eat, Mark?" She gave him her business smile. He was a guest after all, nothing more. Not now.

"I wouldn't mind another cup of coffee. But I'd love some company with it. Do you have a few minutes? You look like you're done with your meeting."

She was finished with Alex and Gina, but there were so many other things on her list today. At least, Macy had volunteered to man the front desk this morning. Could she take a short break? Mark looked so good in his navy Henley and faded jeans. She could enjoy the sights.

"If you don't, I understand," Mark said, his tone disappointed. "It's just I haven't seen you in a while and was hoping to catch up with all you've done since I've been gone."

Of course, it was his fault he didn't know what direction her life had gone in. Aside from a few letters the first year, he hadn't stayed in contact with her. The hurt of him leaving resurfaced and anger skimmed over her nerves. She'd loved him, and he'd taken off with no thought to her feelings. Maybe she hadn't gotten over that yet. Silly, but she wanted him to feel how she'd felt.

Throwing her shoulders back, she tilted her chin up. "I'm

sorry, Mark. I'm far too busy at the moment. But please, enjoy another cup of coffee and pastry. Have a nice day."

She walked out, head held high, and bit her lip to keep from glancing back over her shoulder. She didn't need to. Macy's eyes narrowed as she slid behind the front desk.

"What did you say to him? He looks like you kicked his puppy."

Lord, she was feeling petty. "Well, he kicked mine first."

Macy chuckled and angled so she faced away from the dining room. "That gorgeous man actually ruffled your feathers. I know he's Edele's brother, but there's a story here, and you have got to tell me what it is." Macy had grown up in town, but she was four years younger and probably hadn't been aware that she and Mark had dated.

Kristan took a deep breath and let it out slowly. She was more concerned with how the story was going to end. Doubtful it would be happily ever after.

CHAPTER THREE

Tugging the collar up on his pea coat, Mark shut his car off and glanced around the inn parking lot in the back of the building. He'd had a conversation with Macy today and found out Kristan usually left work around six. Oh, he hadn't been quite so obvious in his quest to know her hours. He'd asked about Macy's brother, Mitch, who'd played hockey with him in high school. Macy had pushed past his subterfuge and given him the details of Kristan's routine and the make, color, and model of her car. If he'd asked, he had a feeling she'd have given him the address and directions to Kristan's house.

So here he was skulking around the parking lot, having gone out and parked next to Krissy when he got back from visiting friends. He didn't want her to think he was stalking her. Even though he basically was.

Something had happened at breakfast this morning, and he wasn't sure what. Yesterday, she'd seemed genuinely happy to see him and possibly interested in catching up. And now he knew she wasn't about to marry Alex Storm, or any guy according to Macy, he had to know what he'd done to close her down.

The back door of the inn opened, and Krissy exited. He needed to time this just right. Waiting for her to get to the edge of the parking lot, he opened his door and got out. He rounded the end of her four-door sedan just as she approached it.

"Hi, Krissy. Heading home for the night?" Yup, appear casual, like this had been serendipitous.

"Oh, Mark." Her hand rose to her chest, then she let out a breath. "I didn't see you there. Have a nice night."

Damn, she wasn't going to engage in small talk. He'd have to take the bull by the horns. "Uh, Krissy, I wanted to ask you something, if you have a minute."

Her eyes narrowed, but she pasted her pleasant business face on again and fiddled with her black and white patterned scarf. "Sure, is there a problem with the room?"

Of course, she'd wonder about that. Business before pleasure. That was his Krissy. Though he'd also managed to get her to engage in pleasure at times when they'd been dating.

"I was wondering if I did something to upset you. You were fairly abrupt this morning when I asked you to join me for a cup of coffee."

She schooled her face and took a deep breath. "I apologize if I was short with you. I can assure you I meant no disrespect. It's a very busy time of the year, and as I told you yesterday, we're down two staff members this week. I've had to pull extra duty and can't be socializing with *guests*."

The emphasis on the word *guests* put him in his place. The idea she didn't even think of him as a friend any longer dug into his heart.

"No, I understand. I'm sorry for whatever I did to make you upset with me."

Her face hardened and she muttered, "That apology is ten

years too late."

Had he heard her correctly? Ten years? She tried to push past him, but he hooked her arm so they faced each other.

"Ten years? You've been holding a grudge for ten years? For what?"

Kristan sucked in a deep breath, and as she let it out it turned into a puff of fog. "Forget it. It's in the past, and I should be getting home."

"No, Krissy. Obviously, you didn't forget it. Whatever *it* is." He dug in his memory for some slight he'd done to her before he left. Oh, he'd left. Was that it?

Narrowing her eyes, she shook her head. "Seriously? You walked out of my life after spending two years together, and I wasn't even worth enough to ask my opinion."

"Your opinion? On whether I should join the navy?"

She folded her arms over her chest, and her eyes darkened. "You never asked what I thought. Just told me you were leaving. Never thinking I might want to go with you."

"Ah, Krissy." He rested his hands on her shoulders, the aggravated look in her eyes morphing to sadness and regret. "We were so young. You were eighteen and needed to go to college. You were too smart to be a navy wife, and I never would have asked you to follow me around the world."

"Navy wives can't go to college?"

"Of course, they can, but too often they have to pack up whenever their husband does and move someplace new. That wasn't the life I wanted for you."

"No, you wanted me living here in the same old town my whole life while you explored the world. Well, you got your wish. I'm still here running the same family business I was working at back then. I haven't even been out of New England in all this time. So this catching up you want to do, is it to brag to me about all the amazing places you've seen while I get to stare at the gazebo every damn day of my life?"

She twisted away and a sob drifted toward him. Damn, he hadn't planned to make her cry.

"Krissy. God, sweetheart, I am so sorry." Stepping closer, he caught her shoulders and drew her to him, wrapping her in his arms like he'd done every day in his memory. "I didn't want to leave you. But I couldn't be a burden on my parents any longer, and I wanted more than my two-year degree. I should have talked to you about it, but I was afraid if I did, you'd talk me out of joining."

Her head moved back and forth against his chest. "I just wanted to be important enough to be in on the discussion. You just left."

And he'd regretted it so often in his life but telling her that now wouldn't fix anything.

"I know. I'm sorry. But I'm here for at least a few weeks. Is there any way we can start fresh and get to know each other again? Spend some time together? Maybe do some of the things we used to have so much fun doing?"

Kristan pushed against his chest and swiped a hand across her face. Tears glistened in her eyes. "I told you I'm extremely busy with some staff out sick. I don't have time to *reminisce*. What's the point, anyway? You said it yourself, you're only here for a few weeks. So, we get to know each other again. And then what? You walk out of my life one more time? I can't do that again, Mark. I'm sorry."

She turned on her heel and slid into her car. The engine started up, and he jumped out of the way as she gunned the engine yet still drove out of the parking lot sedately. Yup, that was his Krissy. Even fighting mad she couldn't disobey the law.

Her taillights disappeared around the corner, and he felt like his heart had gone with them.

∽

Mark sat at the same table again this morning as Kristan typed away at the computer, updating the newest registrations. Why couldn't he sit on the other side of the room where she wouldn't see him? It'd be much easier to get her work done that way. Work that was piling up because she'd constantly been doing everything Janet and Joan typically did.

Naomi, the college girl who worked weekends, sauntered into the lobby and smiled. "Thanks for letting me pick up extra hours now that I'm on winter break."

"I'll give you as many as you want. I appreciate your coming in during the week to help out."

Naomi held up her hands. "Broke student in debt. Happy for the money."

Kristan gave her the run down on the newest guests, who was leaving, and the small party they had tonight in the function hall.

"I'll just tidy up the breakfast room, then head out back to set up for tonight. If you could keep your eye on it after that, I'd appreciate it."

Naomi nodded, then settled in the desk chair. Kristan took her time walking to the dining area, knowing it had been tidied only a half hour ago. Couldn't be too bad since only Mark and one other group had used it.

Still, she gave a cool smile as she sashayed past and wiped the counter down. After pulling a few more to-go coffee cups from the cabinet, she set them in their holder next to the covers. She could probably use another cup herself. It looked to be a busy day.

As she pivoted, hot beverage in hand, Mark lumbered toward her and blocked her way.

"I know you're busy, Krissy. I wanted to know if there's anything I can do to help?"

She schooled her features, biting back the smug retort

that danced on the tip of her tongue. "We're fine, thank you."

He dipped his head so it was closer, and his manly scent wafted her way. "I'm serious. If there's anything I can help you with, I will."

"I thought you were in town visiting your family. You spend more time at The Inn than anywhere else."

His eyes never left hers. "I like it here. Plus, it's Friday and they're either at work or in school. So what's on the agenda for today?"

"*My* agenda? The function room has to be cleaned and set up for a party tonight. I'll be doing that most of the day. Now if you'll excuse me, I need to get started."

"I can push a broom like a pro."

She twisted her head as she moved past. "What?"

That cocky grin flashed her way. The one he always used when he wanted her to do something out of the norm. "Push a broom. Move furniture. Set tables. Heck, I'm pretty handy in the kitchen as well, though I assume you have a chef for the food."

Was he honestly suggesting she put him to work? Or was it only his way of getting back on her good side? *Let's test it out.*

"If you want to do some menial labor, I've certainly got plenty."

His eyes lit up, and he held out his hand. "Lead the way."

She maneuvered through the halls to the large function room that had been added almost thirty years ago by her grandfather. It had brought The Inn so many more customers. They could fit as many as two hundred guests if they spaced the tables closely together. If someone wanted a dance floor, that number went down. Often, they'd set half of the room as a small chapel and hold weddings here. The space was versatile. Tonight's was an office Christmas party for a local engineering firm.

But as she walked into the space, she thought about how much of a pain it was to rearrange everything.

"What's my first job, Ms. Donahue?" Mark's deep voice sent chills through her. Not because of the cold.

"The tables that are up need to be moved and the floor swept and mopped. Then we need to put twelve of them back. The formation is in the binder over here."

She led him to the small office at the back of the room where she held all her notes and details. Flipping to the correct, plastic-protected page, she pointed. "This is what it needs to look like. Then we'll put tablecloths and centerpieces out, as well as the buffet table and the decorations for that."

"Okay, what's our timeline?"

Kristan showed him the schedule and when each step needed to be completed by in order for things to flow smoothly. She couldn't have it any other way. Her reputation, and that of The Inn, counted on it.

Mark wasn't kidding when he said he could push a broom. The room was swept and mopped in half the time it would have taken her or one of the twins. Within an hour, the tables were up, set, and chairs added around them.

"Oh, hey, you started without me," Sofia Storm called out, looking around the space. "I came a little early figuring you might need me. I even brought some muscle to help."

Behind her, an attractive man with Mediterranean features and coloring waved.

"John, thanks for the extra hand. I had my own helper this morning, too." She waved Mark over.

"Mark is Edele Farmer's brother. He's been in the navy for the past ten years. Mark, this is John Michaels. He moved to town a few years back and has a small carpentry and renovations business. And do you know Sofie Storm?"

The men shook hands, and Kristan kept her eye on how

Mark reacted to the gorgeous blonde woman. He merely nodded and smiled. "Of course, I know Sofie. I played hockey with her brother, Greg. I was also in school with some of her cousins. Nice to see you again."

"The place looks great, Kristan," Sofie said as she glanced around the room. "I've got all the Christmas decorations and extras the company asked for. Why don't you take some time off while John and I get the place jazzed up?"

"Oh, I—"

"That's a great idea, honey." Her father walked up behind her and pecked her cheek. "You've been putting in some serious hours lately. Plus, I know you. You'll want to be here throughout the entire event in case any little thing goes wrong."

"Well, someone's got to be here to supervise." Did he expect her to not have an employee, specifically a manager level person, at a big party?

"Right. So, go do something fun now. Something that doesn't involve The Inn."

Her whole life involved The Inn.

"How about skating on the town green?" Mark suggested, his eyes twinkling. "You used to love skating back in high school."

"Mark, I heard you were back in town." Her dad shook Mark's hand and gave him a genuine smile. "Good to see you again."

What? Why wasn't Dad angry at the man who had broken his daughter's heart? Did her dad even realize how much it had hurt her when Mark left? Doubtful, because Kristan was always a stoic little soldier and had pulled herself together and pushed the pain deep inside. Unfortunately, where it had festered for ten long years.

"Have fun," Sofie said, then dragged John away to get her supplies.

"Skating, Krissy?" Mark at least had the decency to ask and not assume she'd go. Which she wouldn't.

"There's too much work to do around here."

"Nope, I forbid it." Her dad laughed. "If you're going to be here late with the party, then you need time to yourself."

Tipping her head, she glared at Mark. "Then, I'll do something at home. Besides, I don't have any skates."

"Your old pair are hanging in the barn at the house. Mark, make sure she doesn't do anything work related for at least another five hours."

"Five hours, Dad? But that's five-thirty. The party starts at seven, and someone's got to make sure Chef has everything he needs."

"And I'll be here to do that. Don't hang your old man out to dry just yet, honey. I've still got a few good working years in me."

"Oh, I know you do, Dad. I just…"

It was useless arguing with her father once he'd made up his mind.

"Thank you, Mr. Donahue. I'll make sure she has fun."

Like Mark could guarantee that. Sure, they might have fun, but then what? He'd go off and leave her again. Like he'd done before.

"Fine. Let's go." She took off marching across the room and slipped into her office to get her purse. Mark tagged along behind.

"I don't need a babysitter. And I'm not sure about skating. I haven't been in years. I'll probably fall and break my leg. That would be perfect timing right before all our Christmas events."

Mark took her arm and led her outside. "I'll make sure you don't fall. And if you do, I'll be right there to catch you."

CHAPTER FOUR

Tugging on her rattiest jeans, Kristan fumed. She didn't want to go skating with Mark. Okay, that was a lie. She wanted desperately to spend time with him but didn't want to be hurt again. But fine. If he wanted to make himself feel better seeing that she was okay and over him, then she could certainly put on a good show. She'd been doing it her whole life.

She slipped her feet into a pair of fuzzy boots, grabbed her warm Christmas green mittens, then fished in the closet for her old ski hat. It was bright orange with pink polka dots. Her brother had given it to her when she'd been a teenager saying they could always spot her on the slopes with it on. She hadn't been skiing in years.

The color of the hat clashed terribly with her hair, but maybe Mark would take one look and opt out of being with her. Grabbing her dark blue parka, she slipped it on, then wrapped a brightly colored scarf around her neck. Yup, no one would believe that Kristan Donahue would dress in such mismatched hues.

As she slid into her sedan, the thought of standing Mark up rolled around her mind. It would serve him right. He'd essentially stood her up by leaving for the navy after dating exclusively for two years. She'd even allowed him to…well, never mind that, she'd wanted it, too. But she might have pushed it off if she'd known what he was planning.

The trip to her parent's farmhouse only took a few minutes and again she debated if she should go or not. Her skates hanging on a nail on the wall of the barn brought back so many memories. Really good memories. Maybe she could allow herself this one indulgence today, then go back to being the staid and upstanding citizen she typically was tomorrow. Or actually tonight, once she got back to work.

When she pulled down the street that led to the parking lot behind the Inn, Mark stood waiting on the corner. Had he known she might change her mind? She never had when she was younger. Very rarely did now. Once she made a decision, she stuck to it. But she'd been shanghaied by her father with this one.

Although, he had a point. She spent so much time at work that doing anything fun was a rarity. Yeah, she and her high school girlfriends went down to the Granite Grill once or twice a month on a Friday or Saturday night to have a few drinks. But only if she didn't have an event she needed to supervise, and she was always on call if anything happened.

Mark waited for her in the parking lot as she exited the car and locked it. There wasn't much crime in tiny Squamscott Falls, but The Inn got people from all over, and it wasn't like they ran background checks before booking them a room.

"You look nice and warm. Ready to go?" Mark's skates hung over his shoulder, and he wore a warm hat and gloves along with his pea coat.

"I guess. But I'm warning you, if I fall and break something, you'll be running The Inn for the next month."

His crooked grin lit up his face. "That'd be fun. The inn part, not the breaking a limb part."

She unlocked her trunk, tossed her purse in there, then took out her skates. "I'm not sure how sharp these still are."

Mark took the skates, made sure the laces were tied together, slung them over his shoulder with his, then held out his hand. Did he expect her to take it like nothing had changed in the past ten years?

"I can carry my own skates."

Taking her elbow, he started walking. "I know you're perfectly capable of doing anything you set your mind to, but humor me and let me pretend to be a gentleman today."

Kristan held her tongue and strolled alongside Mark until they reached the town common, which was covered in white powdery snow. The large square in the center had been shoveled clear and sprayed with water to make the ice for skating. They'd been doing this here for as long as she could remember. It held good memories for her.

Mark found an empty bench and guided her to it. As she removed her boots and slipped on and tied her skates, she looked around. It wasn't crowded yet, but there were lots of familiar faces. Maybe she shouldn't have thrown together all the brightly colored cold weather gear. Or she could have worn one of those hats that hid your entire face with only little holes for your mouth and eyes. She tucked her hair up inside her hat, wrapped her scarf around the lower half of her face, and pulled her sunglasses out of her pocket. It was sunny after all. Partially.

"Are you on the run from the cops or something?" Mark stared at her strangely.

"Just want to be warm."

"I'll keep you warm if you get too cold." His eyes lit up

with mischief. Boy, she knew that expression well. It always ended with him talking her into something that was a bit more adventurous than she'd like. And yet, each time, she'd had to admit what they'd done had been fun.

Standing up, she tested her shaky ankles. Not too bad. "Let's get this skating thing over with so I can go back to work."

Mark shoved their boots under the bench next to a few dozen other pairs. In Squamscott Falls no one worried about stealing shoes. "Oh, no, I promised your dad you'd do something fun and wouldn't even think about work for five hours."

After glancing at the clock on the town hall tower on the other side of the square, she shook her head. "It's closer to four hours now. And I'll need time to go home and dress back in work clothes for tonight's event."

He took her hand and tugged. "You'll have plenty of time, I promise."

They took a few awkward steps, and she tensed as she placed her foot on the ice. Mark's firm grip gave her the confidence to keep going. Pushing off with her left foot, she glided across the ice on her right. In seconds, muscle memory kicked in and she sailed along the perimeter of the man-made rink.

"Like riding a bike." Mark's deep voice drifted from slightly to her left and behind. "You always were very graceful on blades. Made me look like a rookie."

"Oh, please. You played hockey. You could hip check someone in all that gear and still stay on your feet, skating backwards."

"Yup." Mark twisted and faced her while skating backwards, proving her point. "I remember you having some pretty fancy moves, too."

"Give me a few minutes to get my ice legs before we go for the gold, all right?"

Flipping back around, he took her hand and skated beside her for a few turns around the rink. There was a familiar but comfortable silence as they glided along. Many of the other skaters waved or called out greetings, and Kristan smiled at the thought of the wonderful people in this town. Yes, she'd given Mark a hard time about leaving her behind to stare at the gazebo all day, and she did often wish she could do some traveling, but this town was where she was meant to be. Too bad Mark hadn't felt the same way.

They passed Pete and Molly Storm, Alex's parents, who were holding hands and giggling as they skated. Such a cute couple and still so in love. Her heart thumped loudly and her stomach clenched with envy at their obvious adoration for each other, at the longevity and happiness of their marriage. Now, Alex would be happily married as well. Their oldest, Erik, had gotten married a few years ago, and Sara, the youngest and only girl, had been married this past spring. That left Luke. Kristan had a feeling Pete and Molly would be waiting a long time before the playboy youngest brother took the plunge.

"You seem to know so many of these people. That's nice." Mark glided along beside her, still holding her hand. His expression was hard to read. Was he upset that she wasn't paying more attention to him? Or sad that he didn't know everyone in town anymore? Or simply nostalgic for times long past?

"I've lived in this town my whole life, and my family owns a business here. You knew many of these people once upon a time, too."

His mouth tightened at her comment, but he remained silent. She hadn't meant to make him morose. This was supposed to be fun.

Holding his hand tighter, she started skating backwards and grinned. "Let's make a whip."

She picked up speed and pulled. His eyes filled with excitement as he pushed his legs out and overtook her. "I'll lead and you get people attached. They know you better."

She nodded and reached for the hand of the closest person. It was Molly Storm. "Join in. We're making a whip."

Molly's adorable laugh rang out as she placed her hand in Mark's, then tugged on her husband's. Kristan hung on the end looking for their next addition. Three teenage girls lit up with delight and headed their way. Kristan got them added to where Pete held out his hand, then grasped the last one.

She spotted Alex and Gina gliding closer to them.

"Felix, we need to do this." Gina called out, dragging Alex onto the ice as they passed by. They caught the end, and Kristan laughed at the expression on Alex's face. He did *not* like unplanned activities. She understood all too well, but for some reason she was having fun getting everyone involved.

Several of the Storm cousins were here, and she managed to get Greg and his son, Ryan, hanging on as well. Greg had also played hockey, and she could tell he was using his strength to keep the middle of the whip moving as she coerced more people to join. Mark skated in a large circle, and they had so many people involved. Kristan held hands with a young girl who looked scared to death but was also grinning from ear to ear.

"Just keep your feet pointed in the right direction and hold on tight," she told the girl.

Mark zoomed around the rink and finally managed to catch up to the end. When he was close enough, he moved the circle inward a bit until he snagged her hand. His face beamed with happiness.

"Look at you being all spontaneous and fun. I knew you were still in there."

Yeah, she had been more spur-of-the-moment when she was younger. However, most of it had been because of Mark. She'd wanted to be with him all the time and didn't care what it entailed, so she went along with anything he suggested. But today, creating this whip had been all her. And she was having a blast.

Mark pulled away from Molly Storm and tugged until Kristan was free, then he glided into the middle of the group and started spinning with her. They held hands, facing each other and circled around. Clapping registered around her, but she didn't care. She was somewhere she hadn't been in a very long time.

After a few minutes, Mark drew her closer and wrapped his arms around her waist. The spinning slowed down, and she clung to him. The rest of the crowd dispersed, going back to pairs or small groups, though a bunch of the teenagers had kept the whip moving along the outside of the rink. For Kristan, the world had shrunk to just her and Mark, holding each other liked they'd done so long ago.

"THAT WAS AMAZING, KRISSY." Mark gazed down at the beautiful woman in his arms, wanting nothing more than to keep her there. Forever. Well, maybe not right here on the skating rink, because it got a bit chilly after a while.

Her smile warmed any part of him that had been cold. That and her arms still wrapped around his waist. How many times had he dreamed of holding her this way while lying in his bunk onboard the ship? Far too often.

"It was fun. Thanks for jumping in and taking the lead. You're a much stronger skater than I am."

"Don't sell yourself short. And you managed to get almost everyone involved. Great job."

Her eyes were alight with excitement, something he hadn't seen in her since he'd been back. He'd loved this Krissy so much, and it had torn his heart to shreds to leave her. But he hadn't wanted her life uprooted at such a young age. He figured she'd have moved on and been married with a passel of kids by now like his sister. What did it mean that she wasn't? There wasn't even a guy in her life, according to Macy.

Looking at her now, in her faded, worn jeans that hugged her shapely hips and long legs, he dared hope he could somehow get back in her good graces. What would it take? He'd already gotten further than he'd thought, having her go skating with him today.

As much as he hated to unwrap himself from her arms, he didn't want to move things too fast. "I'll race you."

He pushed off and glided away. A competitive expression exploded on her face, and she tore off after him. Carefully weaving in and out of the crowd, they skated around the rink, sometimes forward sometimes backwards, showing off their now remembered skills. He hadn't been skating in forever either. Not much place to do it aboard a navy ship.

They spent the next hour holding hands, spinning together, and laughing as they glided across the ice. The old Krissy was back and having fun. God, he didn't realize how much he'd missed this. How much he'd loved getting her to unwind and enjoy herself.

His time with her today was growing short, but he wanted to spend some of it deeper in conversation than they could do while skating. He tugged on her hand and led her to the edge of the rink.

"Let's get some hot chocolate. The Boy Scouts are selling it up on the bandstand."

"Mmm, I could use something warm about now."

As they sat on the bench replacing skates with boots, he

said, "You should have told me if you were cold. We could have stopped before now."

She tied her laces together and draped her skates over her shoulder. "No, I was having a ball. It's been forever since I've done anything fun like this."

"Really? That's sad and something we'll need to remedy."

She gazed at him strangely and shook her head as she stood. "Hot chocolate."

When they approached the stand, he saw a familiar face bending over a small child.

"Nathaniel?"

Nathaniel Storm glanced up and smiled. "Hey, Mark, long time no see. How've you been?"

"Not too bad." He tightened his hold on Krissy's hand. "We're here having a little fun before the weekend crowds. I heard you're a hotshot lawyer now. How did you get time off for recreation?"

Nathaniel shrugged. "I have my own law firm. Since it's Friday afternoon, almost the weekend, we're doing the same thing. Tanner isn't crazy about crowds. And he's new at this skating thing. He did okay when he held both our hands."

The little boy with the blond curls was definitely Nathaniel's kid. A petite woman with dark, spiked hair and heavily made up eyes strolled over, her hands filled with cups.

"Here you go, Nate. I had them put in extra milk to cool Tanner's off."

She handed a cup to Nathaniel, then glanced down at a small dark-haired girl next to her, who also held a steaming cup. The resemblance was unmistakable.

"Mark Campbell, this is my fiancée, Darcy, and her daughter, Hope. And this little guy is my son, Tanner. Well, they're *our* children now." He gazed at the woman like she was a precious gem.

Mark nodded at Darcy who wasn't at all what he'd expect in a partner for Nathaniel Storm.

"It's nice to meet you. Do you know Kristan?"

Darcy's expressive eyes lit up, and her mouth twisted to the side. "Oh, yeah, we're besties right now. Nate and I are getting married at The Inn in February, and this groovy lady is making it all happen."

Kristan laughed. "It's my job. I'm happy to help."

They chatted for a bit while the kids sipped their warm drinks, and Mark made sure to exchange phone numbers with Nathaniel to get together again. The more time he spent in town, the more he realized maybe it wouldn't be a bad idea to settle back here.

Krissy laughed at something Darcy said, and his gut tightened. Yeah, another reason staying near Squamscott Falls would be ideal. Krissy had every right not to trust him after he'd bailed on her ten years ago. If only he could convince her to take a chance on him again.

Tanner started rocking back and forth, and Nathaniel scooped him up. "That's our cue to head home." They all said their goodbyes, and the little family trotted off down the street.

"Sorry, I promised you hot chocolate. We got distracted." He took Krissy's hand and proceeded to where the warm drinks were sold.

"I don't mind. Nathaniel and Darcy are an odd couple, but they love those kids and each other." She handed the boy at the counter some money before Mark could get his wallet out. "It's great to see how two people so different from each other can still make a relationship work."

Once upon a time, people had said he and Krissy were very different. She'd helped him be more disciplined, and he'd made sure she took time for fun. Was she thinking how they hadn't made it work? Could they now?

A steaming cup was handed to him, and he shoved a five-dollar bill into the jar on the table. Giving to a good cause was always a nice way to spend money.

They took their drinks and wandered around the shoveled paths on the common. At an empty bench, he tipped his head and they both sat.

"We used to do this at least once a week in the winter when we were dating." Krissy's voice held nostalgia. Were they good memories? Or did she regret that she'd wasted so much time with him when nothing had come of it?

"Are you working tomorrow?"

Kristan narrowed her eyes. "I'll probably check in during the morning, but I've got the rest of the day off. Sunday, too. My dad insisted, since I'm scheduled for Christmas."

"I'm glad your dad looks out for you. I have a feeling you'd eat and sleep at the inn if you could."

Krissy let out a frustrated sigh. "It's not that I want to be there all the time, but it's a lot of work for one person. My dad is still involved, but he really wants to retire so he and mom can travel. They figured Zachary would be my partner in running The Inn, but that didn't really work out, so it's me at the moment."

"I've got to spend some time with Edele and her family over the weekend, but I can probably escape after dinner time. Would you be interested in doing something?"

Krissy looked torn. "Even though I'm off, I'm still on call if something happens at The Inn."

"Then we can just go to the Granite Grill for drinks and a little dancing. It's right down the street if anything comes up."

Her pause made him wonder if she was trying to figure out a way to get out of it without hurting his feelings. Should he give her a way out? He didn't want to.

"If you—"

"That could be fun. I'd like to go. There'll most likely be a bunch of people you know at the grill as well. You can catch up on old times."

"Sounds great." But the only one he wanted to catch up with was sitting right next to him.

CHAPTER FIVE

What was she supposed to wear? Mark was picking her up in ten minutes, and she still hadn't decided on an outfit. Most of her clothes were for work and very professional. Were the outfits she typically wore with her girlfriends too casual for a date? And was this an actual date? She had a feeling Mark thought it was.

And what did she think of that? Skating in the town square had been so much fun. She'd enjoyed every second of it. Mark was still the fun-loving guy he'd been years ago, but there was also a more serious vibe that emanated from him every now and then. Ten years in the military could definitely dull an exuberant nature. Had Mark seen much action? Violence? Killing?

For years, she'd worried about him and how he was, even when she was spitting mad that he'd left her so suddenly with barely any warning. What did she feel for him now?

The attraction was still as strong as ever. Maybe stronger since he'd grown into a vibrant man, all muscled and masculine. And she still enjoyed his company. Yesterday's outing had proven that. Could she simply enjoy his presence for the next week and say goodbye like she'd had to do before?

She might not have a choice.

If only she could make a choice about what to wear. Digging in her closet again, she pulled out a dark green sweater dress that hugged her curves and flipped out right below her hips. It was too short to wear with bare legs, for her anyway. Many of her friends would disagree. Plus, it was chilly out. She slid into a pair of matching leggings and slipped on her brown leather ankle boots.

Staring at herself in the mirror, she did a little dance and swished her hips to make the skirt flip back and forth. Very un-Kristan like, but she deserved to be a little daring at times. She laughed at what her idea of daring was. Covered from head to toe in a thick winter material. Still, it wasn't a pressed suit and white blouse.

Grabbing a brush, she dragged it through her hair and started to pull it up, then stopped. Daring. She rolled her eyes. Okay, just not a bun. She combed a bit from each side and attached it at the back of her head with a shiny barrette, allowing the rest of her hair to fall down her back. Mark had always liked playing with her hair.

A little mascara, a touch of blush on her pale cheeks, a soft shade of lipstick that didn't clash with the color of her hair, and she was ready. Lights shone on the street and a car pulled into her driveway. Mark was punctual as usual.

Shutting the lights off in her bedroom, she trotted down the hallway and pulled out her winter dress coat just as the doorbell rang. When she opened the door, Mark stood there, freshly shaven and smelling deliciously of something masculine that reminded her of the forest.

"You look great, Krissy. Ready to go, I see." His gaze roamed her outfit and landed on the coat she held.

He helped her into her outerwear, then glanced around the front hallway. "Is this your house or do you rent?"

Pushing her shoulders back, she nodded. "I bought it last year, once I became manager of the inn and got a nice raise. Paying rent seemed a waste of money. It's not big, but it fits my needs."

"I'm happy for you. It's in a great neighborhood."

As he escorted her to his car, she wondered if he was happy with how his life had turned out. She'd never asked him. Should she? Would it make any difference in the way she thought of him?"

Her house was on the outskirts of town. In nice weather, she was happy to walk the mile and a half to the inn, but December temps made taking a vehicle a better option. When they got close, Mark craned his neck searching for a place to park on the street.

"Why don't you use the inn parking lot? It's Saturday night. Between the skating rink on the common and the restaurants downtown, I doubt you'll be able to find anything available on the street."

"Since I am staying at The Inn, I guess that'd be all right. If not, I know the manager and might be able to sweet talk my way into a spot." He winked as he pulled into the back lot.

Heat crept along her neck at his blatant flirting. Maybe she should pull back a bit. Otherwise, she could find herself in a world of hurt once he left again.

After locking the car, he took her hand and held it close his body. The Granite Grill was on the downtown strip that ran perpendicular to The Inn at the Falls. Often, she'd get take-out for lunch if there weren't leftovers from some event in the function room. The Grill had simple bar food like burgers, wings, and nachos. Regular tables and high tops surrounded the bar area, and if a good song came over the stereo, people used the small area in the middle to boot scoot or hold their baby tight.

"Did you have anything to eat for dinner?" Mark took her coat as she swept the place for an empty table. It was crowded tonight.

"I nibbled on a few snacks, so I'm good. Unless you want to get some appetizers. I'm always up for the nachos here."

"Hmm. Yeah, we can get those. If we can find a place to sit." He frowned when he saw how busy it was.

Her friend, Kelsey, caught sight of her and waved frantically. Next to her was their friend, Ashley, and Gina, Alex's fiancée. Since the house fire at Gina's earlier this year, Kristan, Ashley, and Kelsey, had been making it a point to socialize with the woman when they could. She was lots of fun to be around and made every night interesting.

"I have friends who have some empty seats over there. Did you want to join them or wait until something opens up?"

Mark's frown got deeper. "I guess we can join them. I have to admit I was hoping to have you all to myself tonight."

Leaning in closer, she said, "We can pretend we're all alone on the dance floor when a slow song comes on."

Mark's eyes glowed, warming her even more.

"Hey, Kristan, didn't know you'd be here tonight." Ashley shouted across the table, trying to be heard above the din of the bar.

"It was a last-minute thing." She shrugged, hoping her friends weren't upset she hadn't told them.

"And this is the guy who couldn't keep his eyes off you at the inn the other day." Gina smirked and held her hand out. "I'm Gina Mazelli. Kristan is planning a fabulous wedding for me and my fiancé, Alex, in June."

Most likely, Alex would be planning every last detail and then letting Kristan know. It's how Alex Storm worked.

Mark shook her hand, then smiled at Kelsey and Ashley. "Hey."

"Mark Campbell." Kelsey planted her hands on her hips. "I didn't know you were in town. When did you blow back in?"

Gina's gaze ping-ponged back and forth between her and Mark.

"I got here earlier this week. I'm home for the holidays and staying at the inn since Edele won't stop having kids."

"So you two already know each other?" Gina asked, studying them as only Gina could.

Ashley pointed at Kristan and Mark. "These two were thick as thieves when we were in high school. Quite an item back then. Only stopped because Mark up and joined the navy."

Gina cocked her head. "It all makes sense now."

"What does?" Kristan asked.

"Why you and Felix didn't work out, even though you're perfect for each other."

Mark's hand tightened in hers, and a tiny scowl crossed his face. Was he jealous of Alex? Mark was the one who left her. He had no right to be upset because she didn't sit around pining for him.

Kristan grinned. "I think it was more because Alex has been in love with you, Gina, since you were kids."

Gina's eyes twinkled. "Okay, that too. Well, it's nice to meet you, Mark. Pull up a chair and order us a round."

Mark laughed and waved for Kristan to sit in the empty chair, then scouted to find a free one from another table. When the waitress stopped by, Mark did indeed order a round for the table, plus her nachos and the spicy wings he loved.

Kristan listened as her friends asked Mark about what he'd been doing since he left. She'd wanted to know, too, but hadn't wanted Mark to think she was interested or cared. But she did care. And when his mouth got tight and he gave vague answers, she knew he'd seen some things that haunted him.

Mostly, he talked about the places he'd been to. Some great, some not so great. He elaborated on the great ones and swiftly changed the subject with the bad ones.

After munching on The Grill's excellent nachos, Kristen excused herself to wash up in the bathroom. Kelsey followed her in.

"So you and Mark are picking up where you left off ten years ago, huh?" Her friend's face wore a confused expression. Yeah, Kelsey knew how heartbroken she'd been and how many nights she'd cried herself to sleep.

"No." Kristan scrubbed her hands ferociously under the water. "He's a guest at The Inn. That's all."

"Yet you went skating with him in the common today and are here with him tonight. And looking quite sassy and sexy, I might add."

Kristan rolled her eyes. "I'm wearing a sweater dress with leggings, for Pete's sake."

"A very sexy, sassy sweater dress that I had to talk you into a few years ago and you only wore one other time."

"I haven't done laundry in a while, all right." Like Kelsey wouldn't see right through that. She did laundry at least three times a week. "Mark wanted to get out and relive some of the local flavor, so I said I'd go with him."

"Is there anything else he wants to relive? Like the night after senior prom when the two of you—"

"No, we haven't gone there, and I don't plan to. He's here for a few weeks at most and then he'll be gone with the wind, just like before."

"So you aren't falling for him again?"

"Of course not." How could she be falling for him *again*

when she'd never unfallen? Was that even a word? And why did she have to realize she was still head over heels in love with him in the bathroom of a local bar and grill?

Twisting so Kelsey didn't see the tears that sprang to her eyes, she shoved her hands under the water and rubbed, then realized she'd already done that.

Kelsey chuckled but her eyes held sympathy. "Oh, God, things are that bad so soon. Sweetie, what do you plan to do?"

She shook her head and squeezed her eyes shut, holding those stupid tears at bay. "I don't plan to do anything. I'll simply enjoy his company while he's here, then say goodbye when he leaves. What else can I do?"

Kelsey smirked and her eyes lit up. "You could convince him to stay."

MARK WATCHED as Krissy meandered back from the ladies' room with Kelsey behind her. He couldn't take his eyes off her. She was covered everywhere, except her hands, neck, and head, yet that dress sent his blood pressure skyrocketing. He loved her long, slender fingers with the perfectly painted nails. Not the fake ones that looked like claws but not bitten down either. Just the right length. And her long red hair cascaded down her back tonight, begging him to run his fingers through its silkiness. He wouldn't even think about her neck and the sounds she always made when he'd kissed her there. Not in a public place.

There was a different look in her eyes as she glanced at Kelsey, then swiveled back toward the table. A slow song started on the speakers, and Kristan ran her hand down his arm and smiled. "You mentioned something about getting me on the dance floor earlier."

Actually, she'd been the one to offer the solitude of dancing to a slow number. No complaints here. He took her hand and excused himself from the other ladies.

Several other patrons vied for space on what served as a dance floor. Leading Krissy to the edge, he drew her into his arms, wondering how close she'd allow him. In the past few days, she'd gone from warm to cold back to warm again. What would it take to get her to hot?

Time and patience, if he knew her. And then maybe not even that with the way he'd left.

"Thanks for coming with me tonight, Krissy. It's nice catching up with old friends." Ashley and Kelsey were *her* friends, though he'd hung out with them often during their high school years.

"It's even nicer being alone with you holding me."

Her soft voice practically purred, setting his stomach rattling with nerves. Her fingers caressed the nape of his neck sending shivers through him. Okay, he hadn't expected the hot to show up this quickly, but Krissy was undoubtedly sending him some seriously sexy vibes.

Deciding to take advantage of her playful mood, Mark eased her in closer, his hands smoothing the material over her back and hips. Having Krissy in his arms had been his nightly dream for so many years, it felt right and comfortable doing it now. Maybe he was still dreaming, and he'd wake up to find himself in his bunk on board the ship. God, he hoped not. Not for a long time, anyway. This was perfect.

"I've missed you, Krissy." The words slipped out near her ear, the only indication she'd heard a slight misstep. Soon, she swayed to the rhythm of the music again, brushing against his overheated body.

The song ended and segued into another sultry dance number. Their bodies continued to move without missing a beat. Completely in sync with each other, like they'd been so long ago. Almost as if they'd never been apart.

"Why did you stop writing to me?" The sadness in her tone couldn't be missed, and the fact he'd hurt her stabbed him in the heart.

"I could blame it on my new position on board the ship and all I had to learn, but that would be lying to you and fooling myself. I guess I didn't want you hanging on, not moving on with your life. I had a lot of years to serve and didn't feel it was fair to ask you to wait around for me to come back. I'm glad you didn't."

Now, that was a lie. When he'd heard Kristan was dating Alex, it had killed him. Mostly because he knew Alex was the ideal guy for her. They both had that organized lifestyle and structured way about them. Mark knew they would be happy together. Of course, he hadn't known Alex had Gina in his past, waiting for him to smarten up and realize his feelings. Mark had always known how much he'd loved Krissy, still loved her, but he'd been trying so hard not to be selfish.

Yet here she was still single and unattached to anyone. It didn't seem fair, and he couldn't help but be elated that perhaps he'd been given a second chance. Would he blow it again?

"You're glad I dated other people? Is that what you mean by moving on? It didn't get me very far though, did it? I'm still here in this small town working the same job I had in high school."

"I'm sorry, Krissy, so sorry I left the way I did. I thought I was doing you a favor by not asking you to choose between your family and me."

"Guess you'll never know what I would have decided to do. But that's all in the past. Now, you're here, and we can enjoy the short time we have together. Let's not ruin it."

The music turned to a fast country number, and Krissy

immediately began to bop to the music, shaking her head and swinging her hips. More people crowded the dance floor, pushing him closer to Krissy. She grabbed his hands, swung under them and around, so her back nestled to his front, and continued dancing. It was easy following her steps to the beat, but her proximity set alarms off in him. Ones that said he'd be burned if he stayed too close. The feelings and emotions from ten years ago had risen to the surface, but if Krissy didn't forgive him, he'd be back to dreaming about her instead of holding her.

When the song ended, Krissy whirled around. "Oh, my God, that was so much fun. But I need a drink. Can you get something for me, please?"

"Sure." When he swiveled to go, Krissy jumped into a line dance with her friends.

At the bar, he held up his hand. Logan Osborn, a guy he'd gone to high school with, bounced over.

"Hey, Mark. Good to see you again, man. How've you been?" They shook hands, and Mark ordered a glass of wine for Kristan and a beer for himself.

"I've been good. Edele told me you manage this place now. Nice. Business looks great."

"Yeah, Friday and Saturday night we get a big local crowd. During the week, we do a pretty good lunch and dinner service, and with the common all decked out in Christmas finery, the tourists stop by throughout the month."

"You married yet? Kids? Anyone special?" Mark asked. Logan had been on the hockey team with him and they'd hung out often.

Logan shook his head. "Nah, been too busy getting this place in shape. The owners had let some stuff slide over the years. I've been putting in a ton of time to get the Grill back to where it used to be. How about you? I saw you two-stepping with Kristan out there. I always wondered why no one scooped her up after you left."

"We're catching up again. Not sure where it'll go. At least she isn't seeing anyone right now, so I don't feel like an interloper."

Logan quirked one eyebrow. "I don't remember Kristan dating all that much. She's a workaholic, from what I hear, but she comes in here every so often with girlfriends for a drink and a few laughs."

"She takes pride in her work. But since she's playing now, I need to get this drink to her. Nice talking with you."

Logan asked for his number and plugged it into his phone. Another buddy he could catch up with if he was in town.

Krissy had returned to the table, but her friends still gyrated on the dance floor.

"Here you go. Do you need anything else?"

Krissy sipped her wine, then replaced the glass on the table and leaned near him. "A slow song, so I can have you hold me again."

Mark's breath hitched and his heart sped up. Was this the wine talking? It was only her second glass, and she'd had food to sop up the alcohol.

Taking a drag of his beer gave him time to contemplate her comment. When he lowered the drink to the table, he took her hand and leaned in, too. "I'll hold you as long as you want me to."

"You won't be in town that long." Her sigh echoed his way as she sat back and picked up her wine again. Had she meant for him to hear that?

They spent another hour dancing, catching up with friends, having a good time. His buddy, Greg Storm, who'd also been on the hockey team with him, had shown up with his cousins, Luke and Kevin. The two younger Storms immediately went on the prowl for available women, but Greg, who had a kid at home, seemed content to sip on a beer and chat with people.

Mark managed to get Krissy in his arms a few more times, but she also let loose on the dance floor with her girlfriends. It was great seeing her wilder side, if you could call having fun wild. Krissy had always been far too serious.

When it got late and the place started clearing out, they said goodbye to Ashley, Gina, and Kelsey and made their way to The Inn parking lot.

The lights on the town square sparkled, making colored reflections on the white ground. A few snowflakes fluttered softly around them as they strolled past. He'd forgotten how magical winter in New England could be.

"This is so beautiful. The perfect place to spend Christmas."

Kristan snuggled into his arm as she glanced around. "It is. Perfect." She gazed up at him as she said the last word.

He hated for the night to end, especially as Kristan was sending him signals that she'd happily prolong the evening. But soon enough he'd parked in her driveway and escorted her to her door.

Krissy reached in her purse for her key and inserted it in the lock but made no move to go in once the door was open.

"Thank you, Mark. It was lots of fun tonight."

"Hopefully, we can have more fun while I'm here."

Her lips turned down at his words, so he leaned in and pressed a soft kiss on them. Her eyes drifted closed and she tipped forward. As much as he'd love to stay here kissing her, he knew it wouldn't be right leading her on.

He was only here for a short time. His stay at The Inn was booked until the day after New Year's. Then, he had a decision to make, and Krissy was the key to helping him decide where he went from here. But he didn't think she was ready to hear that yet.

Easing away, he stroked a finger down her cheek. "Good night, Krissy."

Slowly, she backed into her house, and he shuffled down the now slippery, snow-covered walkway. He had some work to do and only eleven days in which to convince Krissy he was worth holding onto and trusting again.

CHAPTER SIX

Kristan finished printing the receipts for all the guests checking out this morning and left them in the folder tucked in the tray to the left of the computer. Naomi was due in any minute, which would give her some time to complete every other task she'd put in her planner today.

The door to her right opened, and Mark strolled through, whistling. He grinned at her, winked, then continued to the breakfast room.

She wasn't sure what to make of that. Saturday night, they'd gone out and had a great time. Kelsey had even convinced her to up her game, to see if she could get Mark to consider sticking around town longer than his original two weeks.

But apparently pressing against him when they danced and running her fingers along his neck didn't do as much as she thought they might. When he'd brought her home, all she'd gotten was a sweet kiss. Granted, it made her lips tingle and filled her with all the emotions she'd attempted to forget over the years, but Mark hadn't prolonged it like she'd hoped. Maybe it was just as well. If he had his mind made up to leave, she couldn't stop him. She hadn't dared ask how long he still owed the navy.

When Naomi showed up and Kristan had filled her in on what needed to be done, she took a detour into the breakfast room to take inventory of what they still had left.

"Good morning, Mark. Did you have a nice time with Edele and her family yesterday?" He'd mentioned they were taking the kids sledding down Parson's Hill for the day and stopping for mulled cider and cider donuts afterward.

"We did, thanks, though I have to admit my legs are a tad sore from climbing that hill a few dozen times. It didn't help that the youngest, Aeryn, wanted me to carry her most of the time."

Kristan laughed, imagining Mark trudging up the hill with a little girl on his back. "You're a good uncle."

"I don't see them much, so I try to be when I'm here. What's on your agenda today?" He slipped the last bite of apple strudel in his mouth and washed it down with coffee.

Pointing to his plate, she said, "I need to see about replacing what you just ate. I get our pastries at Sweet Dreams downtown." She preferred to buy her food locally if she could, so she supported the people in the area.

"That's fairly new, isn't it? I saw it on my walk the other day but didn't go in."

"Yes, my friend Kelsey owns it. She bought out the country store that was in there and changed it to a bakery and candy store. But she's kept the old-fashioned feel to the place. Did you want to take a walk with me and see it?"

Mark smiled. "I'd love to. Maybe I could even sample more of their baked goods."

She nodded at the jacket he'd draped over the chair next to him. "I just need to get my coat and purse. I'll meet you by the front door."

After shrugging on her coat and slinging her purse over her shoulder, she moseyed through the lobby enjoying the way Sofie Storm had decorated it for the holidays. The woman had a natural ability to make places fresh but cozy.

"So this trip is all official business, then?" Mark asked as she joined him.

"For the most part. I love walking downtown and seeing what the shops have done for Christmas. We have a small holiday party tonight for a local business, so I figured I'd take some time now to stroll along the main drag and take in the sights."

Mark opened the door and waved his hand in front of him. "After you."

As they walked along, he loosely gripped her elbow, on the pretense of making sure she didn't slip on the freshly fallen snow. The sidewalks had been scraped clean and covered with a mixture of sand and salt. The town was extremely cautious when it came to the safety of its people.

They passed the Granite Grill, and Kristan led them through the door of Sweet Dreams. On the right, the storefront had been left all exposed beams and homemade shelves holding small wooden barrels of candy. Old-fashioned metal scoops sat in each barrel encouraging customers to dig in and take as much as they wanted. Small paper bags rested on the end of each row for the candy to go in. A hanging metal scale swung from the ceiling so people could weigh their spoils.

The surrounding shelves held boxes and bags of homemade mixes from local producers. Soups, muffins, and breads mingled with jams, jellies, spreads, and sauces in cute glass jars.

"I should get a little candy for the kids. Do you mind if I take a few minutes?" Mark indicated the small barrels.

"Go ahead. I need to talk to Kelsey about an order."

Her friend stood behind the counter on the left, tucking a half dozen cupcakes into a box for a mother and her two children. Once Kelsey rang up the purchase, she tucked her dark hair behind her ears, and blew the wispy bangs out of her face.

When the family had left, Kristan stepped forward and smiled. "Busy day?"

"We've had a steady crowd. More so earlier this morning for the breakfast pastries, but for a Monday, it's been good so far. Do you have a final head count for the party tonight?"

Kristan pulled her list from her purse and handed it over. "You'll see the number of each dessert we want for tonight. But I also want to make sure you get the breakfast order for the next week. It's all right there. We're booked solid, and guests have been taking a muffin or pastry with them as they head out for the day. I want to add a few special orders for some incoming guests who have allergies and increase the amount of goods to make sure we have enough."

Kelsey smiled. "Always happy to provide more. Let me just get this to Luci, so she can start working on tonight's batch."

Kelsey marched into the back. Mark appeared at her shoulder holding four tiny paper bags filled to the brim with candy.

"Just a *little* something for them?"

Mark's sheepish grin transformed his face and made him look twenty again. And it brought back too many bittersweet memories. Turning away, she saw Luci Storm saunter out behind Kelsey.

"Oh, my goodness. Mark Campbell?" Luci called out. "I haven't seen you in ages. Oh, the times you and Greg used to tear up my house. Thick as thieves during hockey season. Are you here to spend Christmas with your sister?"

Mark smiled. "I am, except I'm staying at The Inn. I'm

escorting Kristan as she runs a few errands. I thought you worked for The Muffin Shop over in Stratham."

Luci grinned. "When Kelsey opened this place up, she enticed me away. It's closer to home and better hours, so I can be there when Greg's son, Ryan, gets back from school. Plus Kelsey lets me have more say in what I can bake."

Kelsey's eyes opened wide. "Her recipes are amazing. Some of them have turned into bestsellers."

"Like that apple strudel you enjoyed so much this morning." Kristan pointed to the desserts in the glass case next to them. "And those cinnamon rolls you devoured the last few days."

"I thought those tasted familiar, Mrs. Storm. You used to make those for us at the beginning of hockey season every year. And again if we made the playoffs."

Luci winked. "I would have made them even if you hadn't made the playoffs. But you always did. You boys were formidable as a team."

Mark puffed up and grinned. "Yeah, I caught up with Greg at The Grill Friday night. We're hoping to make plans to get together again."

"I hope you do," Luci said. "I love watching my grandson, especially now that we don't live in the same house. Greg needs to get out and socialize more. Maybe find himself a nice girl. It's been too long."

The store grew quiet as they remembered how Greg's wife had died only a few months after giving birth to Ryan. Mark cleared his throat and placed the candy bags on the counter.

"I can help with the socializing, but finding a girl he'll have to do on his own."

Luci gave Mark a big hug. "Don't be a stranger." Then, she headed into the back room.

Would Mark go back to being a stranger in his own

hometown? All this talk about getting together with old buddies...was it just talk? Or would Mark make an effort to stay in touch with his friends? With her?

"Can I get you anything else?" Kelsey asked Mark as she rung up his purchases.

Mark studied the cupcakes, frosted cookies, cannoli, cinnamon rolls, and other pastries displayed in the case. He peeked at her. "Can I talk you into something sweet while we're here?"

Kelsey stared at her curiously. Okay, Friday night she'd denied any relationship with Mark to her friend and now she was hanging out around town with him. She might as well give everyone something to talk about.

"I guess I wouldn't mind a cinnamon roll with another cup of coffee. I only had one this morning and it's been hours."

Mark ordered coffee and another apple strudel, and they took them to one of the small bistro sets near the window on the bakery side. Kelsey had really done a beautiful job of making this place cozy and inviting.

As they sat talking, several more townsfolk wandered in, greeting both she and Mark. Seemed he still knew many of the locals, even though he'd mentioned feeling like an outsider when he first got back.

"What's our next stop?" Mark asked as they finished their food and tossed the trash in the basket.

Waving to Kelsey, she proceeded him out of the bakery. "Serendipity is next door."

"Do they still sell all local artisan crafts?" Mark gazed in the window.

She nodded. "They've expanded to add local wood crafters with some unique furniture. The coffee table in the lobby of The Inn was made by a man who lives out on Exeter Pond."

She and Mark browsed through the cards and jewelry, then admired the paintings, fabric goods, ceramics, and glass figurines. He picked out one depicting a mother reading to her children and had the clerk wrap it in festive paper for him.

"Edele is such a good mom. I'm not sure how she does it. Especially with four. I often wonder how good of a parent I'll be."

As they shuffled outside to the sidewalk, she asked, "Do you want children?" It was something they hadn't talked about when she was a teenager, though she'd always assumed one day she'd have some.

He stared across the road at the common where parents chased after their kids and skated around the rink. "I do. I guess I never really thought about when, though. Sometime in the future. But I'm already thirty years old."

"That's not old. I'm twenty-eight and don't have kids yet. Many of my friends don't."

He swiveled quickly toward her and placed his hands on her shoulders. "Do you want children?"

Why was he asking? Did he want them with her? Or was she putting meaning in his words that wasn't there?

"I do, yes. But I haven't found the right man to have them with yet." Well, she had, but he'd skipped town and hadn't kept in touch.

"A little girl with long red hair and freckles just like you." Mark's eyes crinkled with laughter. "I can picture it now."

But who did he picture as the father? Him? Or was he still planning to walk away and let her find someone else to have those kids with? She was beginning to think she'd never find anyone for that job. Not when all she could think about was Mark.

"The next place down is The Book House." Best veer away from that subject for now. "Did you want to go in?"

Mark nodded. "They always had a nice selection of reading material. Not that I've had much time to read since I've been here."

They walked around the store, and when they got to the alcove where the children's section was, Mark stopped and cocked his head. "Didn't this space used to be Hofstetter's Jewelry Store?"

"It was until recently. It's a long story. Just don't ask Gina or Alex." She shook her head at that town scandal. "The Book House took over the space, and now this smaller store is called The Book Mouse and has only children's books."

Mark nodded. "I should get the kids some books, but I'm not sure what they read. Maybe I can ask Edele and come back here later."

"Have you not shopped for them yet?" She was the type of person who had all her Christmas shopping done in September and wrapped before Thanksgiving.

"Oh, I have their presents, but that whole not seeing them thing makes me want to buy them more."

They meandered about the store, and Kristan picked out a nice calendar for her kitchen wall at home. She'd already purchased her desk calendar for work months ago. Mark pulled out his phone and texted a few times, then selected some books for different age groups. Edele must have helped him.

After leaving that store, they crossed the street and wandered through a few more. Mark turned into a kid when they hit Shenanigans. The toy and novelty store had so many gadgets to play with on display, it was a wonder they had space to store their stock.

Glancing at her watch, Kristan realized it was after noon. She'd need to get back to The Inn in about an hour to make sure everything was all set for the event tonight. However, lunch would be nice.

"Are you hungry?"

Mark replaced the electronic dog that barked and wagged its tale on the shelf and threw her that boyish grin again. "Yeah, I could go for some food. Do you need to get back to work?"

"In a bit. The Loaf and Ladle is a few doors down. They've still got the best soups and sandwiches around and its quick."

Holding his arm out for her to take, he said, "It would be my pleasure."

They walked out of the store and down the street, calling to people around them as they passed. But if Mark planned to leave town at the end of his time here, would she still think this time with him had been a pleasure?

CHAPTER SEVEN

The inn lobby smelled of pine, and Mark paused near the live Christmas tree in the corner to indulge in the scent. This was what Christmas was supposed to smell like. Not salty beach and sunblock like the years when he'd been stationed someplace tropical. It made him want to put down roots here in this small town. The other factor for wanting roots here stood behind the front desk across the room. Her gorgeous hair was down again, with only a shiny clip holding back one side.

Kristan looked up, and her whole face glowed. From seeing him? God, he hoped so. Seeing her, being with her this past week, had helped him clarify what he wanted to do in life. Or maybe he should say where he wanted to do it. Finding a job that could support him, and any other family he might have, was a whole different story. Small towns were great but didn't have tons of opportunity. Of course, the other towns in the area, even Portsmouth, might have different possibilities. Once the holidays were over, he'd have to take a serious look at what was available around here.

"Hey, Mark, what've you been up to this morning?"

"I spent some time with my sister and her family. The kids are beyond excited for Santa to come down that chimney tonight."

"Ah, the magic of the holiday. Are you heading back there tonight for Christmas Eve?"

He shook his head. "No, they're heading to Jay's family for dinner and celebrating."

Kristan's face fell and her lips tightened. "Oh, and you aren't going with them?"

"They invited me along, but Jay's parents live a few hours from here, and I'd have to sit way in the back of the minivan for the trip. Then, Jay is one of six kids and all his nieces and nephews will be there. I love kids, but I draw the line at a dozen of them hyped up on candy and Santa in an enclosed space. I need to keep my sanity for at least another week."

Kristan laughed. "I guess I understand. What do you plan to do?"

He'd thought of calling one of his old buddies from high school, but both Greg and Nathaniel had kids now and Logan was working tonight. A muscle ticked in his jaw and he shrugged.

"Maybe I should have gotten a book at the bookstore yesterday. I think they're still open, so I could run over now."

Kristan moved from behind the desk and sidled right up to him. When she touched his arm, it sent his nerves into overdrive. She'd always had that effect on him, and nothing had changed. Well, maybe Krissy's feelings for him had changed.

"We're having a small dinner at my parents' tonight. It's just them, me, and my brother, Zachary. I'm sure they wouldn't mind if you tagged along."

He'd always gotten along with Krissy's family but wasn't sure what they thought of him now. Her father had certainly been cordial enough the other day when he'd seen him. But was Kristan merely asking out of pity?

"It's fine. You don't need to find something for me to do. I'm a big boy and can handle being alone for a night."

Her eyes narrowed, her lips twisting to the side as her gaze swept him from head to toe. "Yes, you are a big boy. One I'd love to have accompany me to my parents' house this afternoon."

"I don't want to intrude, but I appreciate the offer. Your parents aren't expecting to feed another mouth."

"I'm bringing some of the dishes, actually. Didn't you say you were handy in the kitchen? I could use a hand getting the casseroles ready. I've got to work until three. It doesn't leave me much time to get home, throw the food together, cook it, and still jump in the shower and become beautiful."

Reaching out, he stroked a finger down her porcelain cheek. "You're always beautiful, Krissy. It isn't something you have to work at."

"Still, I could use a hand putting the meals together. Or were you telling tales when you said you were good in the kitchen?"

He'd done a good deal of KP duty when on board his ship. His shipmates had never complained. "Okay, I'll help. Do you need me to pick up anything at the grocery store?"

"I do have a couple things I forgot. If you went now, I wouldn't have to waste time after work."

"Give me a list, and I'll go. What time do you want me at your house?" He glanced at his watch. It was two-twenty-five.

"Why don't I give you my key, so you can put the supplies in the fridge if you get there before I do?"

Mark remained silent as he nodded. Krissy trusted him enough to give him the key to her house. She moseyed her way back to the front desk, pulled a slip of paper from her planner, dug for her keys, and handed them to him.

"Keep the receipt and I'll reimburse you when I get back. Thanks so much."

He glanced down at his dark gray chinos and burgundy shirt. "Is this okay or should I change?"

She gave him a thumbs up. He squeezed her hand, then left her standing there staring after him. All the way to the grocery store and then to her house, he wondered at Krissy's feelings. Should he ask? When he first got here, she'd been very blunt about the fact he'd hurt her and she didn't have time in her life for him now. But the recent days, she'd softened her stance. Not pushing him away, yet she hadn't exactly been declaring her undying love.

You haven't either.

Good point. But was Krissy ready for that? He loved her, and the more time he spent with her, the more he knew coming back to this town and attempting a relationship with her was the right thing. But if he hadn't proven himself to her yet, was telling her his feelings going to make everything explode? How could he tell when she was ready?

Letting himself in, he decided he would spend the time he had left trying to earn her trust and her love back. Before he checked out of The Inn, he'd let her know how he felt. And pray that she felt the same way.

A little after three, Krissy walked in, her arms filled with bags. He rushed over to help her.

"What's all this? I thought you only needed the stuff on the list you gave me?"

After dropping a few on the kitchen table, she shrugged off her coat. "These are gifts from my staff. I tell them every year not to get me anything, but they always do."

"Do you get them gifts?"

"Of course I do, but I'm their boss. They all work

extremely hard at their jobs. They deserve a little something extra at the holidays."

Mark took her coat from her and draped it over a chair, then set his hands on her shoulders. "Your staff knows you work hard, too, and they all respect that and how you treat them. Maybe you deserve a little something extra as well."

Krissy rolled her eyes. "How do you know what the staff think of me?"

"I've asked a few of them. Not outright, but in conversation. They all know how much you put into making The Inn a success, how much time you spend making every little detail perfect. Way more time than most managers would."

Krissy stared across the room as a huge sigh left her. "I don't really have much of a choice. I'd love to hire an assistant, but I don't want my dad to think I can't do the job."

When he pulled her to his chest, she didn't even resist. Was there a way he could reduce her stress? Aside from hiring her an assistant manager? Her entire body sagged against him, and he tightened his hold and pressed a kiss to her hair. This was what he wanted. To hold the woman he loved when she needed him.

Too soon, she was easing back, but with a more relaxed smile. "As much as I'd love to stand here letting you hold me, I have a few casseroles to put together before I can even think about a shower and changing."

"What did you plan on making? Do you have recipes you follow?"

Krissy slid a plastic sheet protector across the center island and showed him. "The meatballs are already in the crock pot. I'm also making chicken, broccoli Alfredo. I haven't made it before, but this one looked easiest. And I'm in charge of making these little crabmeat, English muffin things for an appetizer."

He perused the recipes cards and nodded. "These look

simple enough." Actually, the Alfredo dish could be improved upon, and he knew exactly how to do it. "Why don't you let me get them started while you go clean up. Do you still love bubble baths?"

Krissy rolled her eyes. "I do, but rarely have time for them anymore. The master bath in this house has an incredible tub with jets and everything. I never get to use them."

"Well, that's your assignment then. Fill the tub, put on the jets, and take a long relaxing soak. Leave the cooking up to me."

Her eyes bounced back and forth from the fridge to the stove. "Are you sure?"

"I told you, I'm good in the kitchen. Now go. Relax. Just don't fall asleep and drown. My CPR is a bit rusty."

"Thank you." Her voice held gratitude as she pressed a kiss to his cheek. Pivoting, she snatched one of the bags and swung it back and forth. "Got some great bath salts from the head of housekeeping, but I didn't think I'd get a chance to use them for a while."

As Kristen's sensible shoes tapped down the hallway, Mark pulled out ingredients from the fridge and cabinets. He wouldn't tell her he'd inspected her place before she'd gotten here. It was a cute Ranch house with a huge living room that opened into a sunroom in the back, overlooking the yard. The kitchen had a big dining area and all the modern conveniences you'd need for a large family. The one drawback was it only had two bedrooms. But the yard was large and there was definitely room on the other side of the house for an addition with a couple more bedrooms. If Krissy were ever in need of more bedrooms.

Visions of adorable little redheaded children scampering in the backyard kept him busy while he put together the ingredients for the Alfredo dish, tweaked to make it better. Once that was in the oven, he mixed the crab meat, cheese, mayonnaise, and added some spices. He spread the mixture on the English muffin halves then covered them and put them in the fridge. They'd have to be cooked right before they were eaten. Lifting the lid off the meatballs, he tasted one. Not bad. But he had just the thing to make it a little bit better.

The sound of Krissy moving about in her room drifted down the hall. She'd given herself a half hour in the tub. Not as long as she probably needed but more than he figured she'd allow herself.

Scuttling about the kitchen, he tidied everything up and wiped down the surfaces. When Kristan entered the kitchen a half hour later, decked out in black slacks and a red blouse, the place was back to the pristine room it had been when he'd gotten here.

She glanced around, her brows touching. "Did you start making the food?"

Peeking in the oven, he nodded. "Alfredo needs another ten minutes. Crabbies are ready to pop in the oven at your parents' place. If you need something to get you by until then, you can crack that open."

When he pointed to the object on the counter, her mouth fell open and she cried out. "Oh, I love chocolate oranges. I don't think I've had one since..." Her gaze slipped away. "Since you left."

"I'm sorry. I didn't mean to bring up bad memories. We used to love sharing them. Even before we started dating."

Krissy grinned. "I remember. It's when I first noticed you. I was sleeping over Edele's house, *your house,* the week before Christmas and you had one of these. Edele didn't really like them, and I think your mom was trying to lose weight, so she refused to eat it. You told me we had to do our part to make sure the Christmas spirit of the chocolate orange lived on."

"I did say that, huh? God, I was goofy. And you ended up going out with me later anyway."

Pink covered her cheeks. "I thought you were kind of cute. Even when I was ten. I couldn't believe you wanted to go out with me once I turned sixteen."

"You don't know how hard it was to wait that long, but your parents were pretty strict with you about dating, so I waited. It was worth it."

A melancholy expression crossed her face, and Mark realized he'd stepped in it. Yeah, he'd waited to go out with her, then left her behind after being together for two years. What an idiot.

"Have a piece. You want to crack it or should I?"

Kristan opened the box and took out the wrapped chocolate. Taking a deep breath, she slammed the sweet on the counter.

"Feel better?" Hopefully, she hadn't been picturing his face on the orange.

"I do." Her eyes sparkled as she unwrapped the foil and slid a slice of chocolate into her mouth.

Her moan of appreciation had him swallowing hard and turning away to check the casserole. It was ready.

"Do you have a box to put this in? It's hot."

"I have better than that." She dug under the cabinet and pulled out a fancy thermal container that fit the casserole dish perfectly and had a handle that didn't get hot.

He put the crock pot in the car first, then took the hot dish, while she carried the tray of crabbies. They took her car, since it already had all her presents for her family in it.

On the way, he asked how her family was and if there was anything that had changed since he'd moved out of town. She mentioned her brother and the fact he'd become a marine biologist instead of studying business or hospitality management like she had. There was definite stress in running The

Inn, and Mark wondered how to help ease her burden. But when Krissy talked about the place, she spoke in a loving tone. It was where she needed to be. He wished he had such a clear idea of what he should do.

The only thing clear at this point was that he wanted Krissy back in his life.

CHAPTER EIGHT

Mark skipped down the stairs of The Inn and pushed through the door at the bottom. It was barely eight o'clock, but he knew Krissy was already here. Yesterday, at her parents' house, they'd talked about how she was working a twelve-hour day today, so most of the staff could be home with their families. Krissy had blown it off, but her dad made a point of saying what a good boss it made her.

Diane and Bruce Donahue gladly welcomed him into their home and insisted he take some of the homemade breads and cookies they had to share with his sister's family. If Krissy's parents were upset with him for leaving their daughter ten years ago, they never let on. They asked about his years in the navy and what he planned on doing once he was done. Krissy had listened intently, though she'd never asked him that question herself since he'd been back.

Her brother, Zachary, had an interesting job traveling around doing studies on ocean animals. Even though Krissy smiled and nodded at his tales, Mark could tell there was tension there. Because she hadn't been able to travel? It's what she'd thrown in his face a few days ago.

Nevertheless, the night had been fun, and he'd seen Krissy really relaxed for the first time in a long time. When he'd driven her home, he'd stopped at her door and kissed her good night. He lingered longer than he had Friday night, but still hadn't pushed beyond kissing. He left wanting more but also knowing what that kiss had shown him—the magic when her lips met his was still there. Neither one of them could deny it.

Whistling a holiday tune, he sauntered up to the reception desk and leaned on it. "Good morning and Merry Christmas."

Kristan looked up from the computer screen and gave him a huge smile, then stood. "Good morning."

He took advantage of her closeness and stole a kiss. "It's even better now."

She rolled her eyes and shook her head. "Are you off to Edele's?"

"Nope. I'm letting the kids get all the present frenzy out of the way. I'll show up in time for the food."

She laughed, and the sound floated like a chime through the lobby. "Help yourself to coffee and pastry in the breakfast room. There's nobody in there right now."

Placing the small gift bag he'd brought down on the counter between them, he winked at her. "You need to open your Christmas present first."

"Mark, you shouldn't have." Her eyes showed gratitude but also guilt. "I didn't get you anything."

"I didn't expect you to. This isn't much. Just a little memory of my being here."

Kristan pulled out the tissue paper, then lifted the ornament up by its ribbon. "A skate. It's so cute. Thank you." She twisted her head, but not before he saw tears well in her eyes.

"Come put it on the tree." He backed away and strode to the tree in the corner.

It took her a moment and a clearing of her throat, but she left the confines behind the desk and strolled across the lobby, holding the ornament as she stared at it.

Mark cupped his chin in his hand and studied the tree. "What do you think?"

Krissy tipped her head and narrowed her eyes. "The perfect spot would be right here in front." She adjusted an ornament that was in the way and placed the skate dead center on the tree.

"Beautiful."

Krissy smiled, then blushed when she saw he was staring at her and not the tree. "Oh, go get some breakfast."

Taking her hand, he drew her close. "There's no one here. Join me. Please."

When her lips pursed and she glanced around the lobby, he thought she'd refuse, but another smile crossed her face and she nodded. "Okay. It's Christmas Day and I'm working, so I guess I should be allowed a little leeway."

"Yes, you should." He followed her into the dining room, and they both got coffee and filled plates with fruit and pastry.

"I need to sit so I can see the front desk." Krissy took his typical place, and he sat across from her.

"How many people are checking out today?"

After sipping her coffee, Krissy answered, "No one. We don't have any new arrivals either. I'm mostly here if any guests need something or have a problem with a room."

They chatted about her parents and where they wanted to travel to once her dad fully retired. About Edele and the kids and the activities and sports they did after school.

"I wish I could be around more to see them. I need to make that a priority."

Kristan stared out the window, her expression conflicted. Finally, she asked, "How much longer do you have in the navy? Or are you planning to make it your life's career?"

"I'm officially done. My discharge papers should be ready in a few weeks." He watched her carefully for her reaction.

"Oh, well, that's uh…" Her voice was breathless, and her brows knit together. "What do you plan on doing now?"

Reaching over, he took her hand. "That depends on a lot of things. I need to find a job first."

It looked like she was holding her breath. "Where exactly did you plan on searching? Or do you know?"

Mark gazed out the window at the gazebo covered in snow, the colored lights peeking out and shining for all to see. "This past week has made me reevaluate a lot of things in my life. Being here, in this town, has brought back tons of good memories. I wouldn't be opposed to settling somewhere in this area. The biggest problem is finding a job that pays enough for me to live on."

"Here? Squamscott Falls? You'd consider moving back here?" Her eyes glimmered. God, had he made her cry again?

"Yeah, maybe. We'll have to see what the future brings."

"That's great." Kristan stood and wiped her hands on a napkin. "I need to check something at the reception desk."

As she clicked across the hardwood floor, he heard a sniff, and she pushed her hand across her cheeks. How did he interpret that? Was she upset he'd be around interfering in her life, or were those happy tears? Did he leave her alone and go back to his room until noontime, or did he push so he could spend time with her like he planned?

He gave it a few minutes, then picked up her plate with half a cinnamon roll still on it and carried it to the desk. "You'll need this if you're going to get through this busy day."

"Thank you, Mark. I do actually have a lot planned for today." Kristan was back and all business.

"Can I hang around for a bit and help you do it? I don't want to be underfoot, but I have no idea how an inn runs. It could be fun seeing what you do. If not, it's okay. I can go back to my room for a few hours."

He tried to make that last sentence sound pathetic, so she'd let him stay around. When she laughed, he knew it had worked.

"Okay, come on back here and sit down."

For the next few hours, she showed him her world. Making schedules for all the staff, which was harder than it looked. She showed him how she did all the purchasing for every aspect of the inn. She got input from housekeeping, maintenance, the event center, and the business office first, but made all the final decisions herself or with her father.

"Luckily, Macy Wagner, our office manager, does all payroll and billing and keeps the books."

Kristan had everything in labeled file folders, placed in specific trays, and easily available. "Once I get the supply list from the head of each department, I need to get vendor quotes. I often use the same supplier once they've proven themselves, but I still like to check the competition every now and again to make sure there isn't a better deal out there. This is one of the things that is so time consuming in my job."

As she typed up e-mails, Mark asked, "Why are you sending those now? Aren't these businesses closed today?"

"They are, but if I send the e-mail now, it'll be there first thing when they come back after the holiday. It's one less thing I'd have to do later. It's one of the reasons I didn't mind working Christmas. I knew I could get all this work done without being bothered by other staff."

"You really should think about hiring an assistant manager. I know you want to prove to your father you can do this job, but I think you've already done that. He couldn't say enough good things about you at the house last night. Is it finances? Does The Inn not make enough profit to support a second manager?"

Krissy sighed. "It does. But you know me. I like to be in control, and the thought of someone else making decisions about this place doesn't sit well with me. It's been family run for over a hundred years. I don't want to change that now."

"And Zachary is busy with his marine animals."

Nodding, Kristan sighed again. "It's okay for now. It's not like I have a husband or kids waiting at home for me. I've got the time to give to The Inn. And I do love this place."

Except he knew Krissy. She'd keep working here and giving this job everything she had. Little by little, her social life would completely peter out because the inn took precedence. What would her life be like then? If he stuck around, would she find time in that life for him? Or would he come in second behind her job?

Or was there another way to help Krissy, so she could keep working the job she loved but also have time for that husband and family she talked about? He'd have to give it a great deal of thought.

"THANK you for keeping me company tonight."

Kristan closed her car door and buckled her seatbelt. "I'm happy to return the favor. You kept me company all Christmas morning. I wasn't expecting that."

She had figured she'd be fairly depressed hanging out at work all by herself during the holiday. And she had once Mark had gone to his sister's. But they'd had fun while he'd been there. She'd been proud showing him what she did for a living and how good she was at it. He hadn't come right out and said, it, but she could tell he'd been impressed.

Mark shifted the car into gear and reversed out of her driveway. Once on the road, she peeked at his profile. Lord, the man was handsome. Even more so now than when they'd dated ten years ago. He took her breath away every time he came near. It wasn't just his looks. Mark had a way of making everyone feel good about themselves. It wasn't that he gave out blatant compliments, but he discussed and asked questions tailored to each person's talents and knowledge. He'd done that with her on Christmas Day.

As they pulled up his sister's driveway, Mark glanced at her. "Last chance to get out of it."

When he'd mentioned babysitting Edele's kids so his sister and her husband could have a date night, she'd laughed and told him to have fun. But, in seconds, he'd charmed her into going with him to help.

"You can still run if you want. It's a few miles back to your house, but you wore your sneakers. You should be okay."

She had worn her sneakers when she realized she'd be hanging out with four children ages four to ten. What had she gotten herself into?

Stepping out of the car, she stared down the driveway. Mark grabbed her hand and dragged her to the house. "Nope, too late to turn back now. You're committed."

"Hopefully, I won't need to be committed after spending a few hours here."

Edele opened the door as they approached and enveloped Kristan in a warm hug. "It's so great to see you again. Mark has really enjoyed spending time with you this week."

Had Mark been talking about her to his sister? What exactly had he been saying? She and Edele had been good friends in high school, but since the woman was now married with four children, they didn't have as much in common and had even less time to socialize. Kristan wanted to drill Edele with questions but never had the chance. In seconds, she was ensconced in the large country kitchen with four little faces staring at her.

"This is my good friend, Kristan, who I grew up with. She runs The Inn at the Falls. You've met her a few times, but I don't know if you remember."

The youngest had been a baby the last time Kristan had seen her, so it was doubtful she remembered.

Mark slung his arm over Kristan's shoulder and introduced the kids. "This is AJ," he said pointing out the tallest boy. "Then Nick, Asher, and the one who doesn't like to climb hills is Aeryn."

The little girl laughed, ran, and threw her arms around Mark's legs. He scooped her up and tossed her over his shoulder. "I think you ate too much for Christmas," Mark scolded in a silly voice. "I hope you don't plan any more sledding this week."

Aeryn giggled again, then squirmed until her uncle slid her to the floor.

Jay tromped into the kitchen and swung keys around his finger. "You rug rats better behave for your uncle and Miss Kristan here or there'll be trouble tomorrow." The man's growly voice was too comical to be scary.

"They'll be fine. Go and have fun." Mark swatted at Edele and Jay, and after kissing the kids, they left, happy smiles on their faces.

The door had barely closed when Nick grinned and bounded over to Mark. "You said blanket fort, right?"

"Oh, yeah," Mark replied. "We can have a little contest to see who creates the best one."

Aeryn's face fell and her lips pushed out. "I don't know how to make one as good as them." She pointed at her brothers.

Kristan stepped closer. "Maybe we could have a girls' team. You and I work together."

Aeryn's eyes lit up, but Asher began to pout. "I have to do it by myself?"

Mark folded his arms over his chest and looked at the two older boys. "How about I provide counsel to Asher, Krissy helps Aeryn, and you two boys get to go solo? Deal?"

AJ and Nick smirked and nodded. In minutes, they had half a dozen sets of sheets and four blankets piled on the family room floor. Mark doled out a blanket and sheet set to each team or person, divvied up the room so everyone had some furniture to drape over, and set some ground rules.

"We have twenty minutes to build the fort. You can use any part of the furniture you want, but you can't rip or break anything, including the sheets. You can move the furniture but no more than two feet in any direction. And you can't do anything to knock down another person's fort. Agreed?"

The kids all agreed, and Kristan hid her smile. If she ever had kids and came home to find a babysitter doing this, she'd have a fit. On the other hand, the way Mark dictated the rules and made sure everything was equal was amazing.

Mark declared the time, then shouted, "Begin."

Kristan studied the reclining chair and the tall bookcase they were given and whispered to Aeryn, "Let's turn the chair around so the front of it faces the bookcase. Then, we can drape the blanket between them. Does that sound good or did you have a different idea?"

Aeryn's little face scrunched up. "I've never made a blanket fort before. I'm glad you came with Uncle Mark, so you could help me."

They got busy arranging the sheet over one side of the chair and kept it anchored to the bookcase with a throw pillow. They threw the blanket over the back of the chair to keep the sheet from slipping off. It formed a snug little area about five feet wide, and you could sit on the chair or on the floor in front of the bookcase.

"This is perfect," Aeryn cried out, her face beaming. "If we had a light, we could read a book."

Kristan ducked out of the enclosure and dug around in her purse. The small flashlight she kept in there for emergencies was exactly what they needed. When Aeryn saw what she had, she clapped and laughed, reaching for a children's book on the bookshelf.

Kristan crossed her legs and sat on the floor in front of the chair, and the little girl snuggled right into her lap as she opened the book. She'd only read the first page when Mark called out time.

"Let's take a look at what everyone did."

After hugging Aeryn tight, she said, "We'll finish this in a minute. We should see what the others did."

The two of them crawled out of the fort. Kristan almost cringed when she saw the family room transformed into a tent city, blankets and sheets everywhere. But the looks on the faces of the children was magical. That's what was important.

One by one, they checked out each blanket fort. AJ's was mostly just under the coffee table, a little too low for Kristan to attempt to get under. Mark got on the floor to examine it, then clowned around like he couldn't get up and needed help. All four children rushed to his aid.

Nick had draped his blankets over two upholstered chairs and had pushed them apart so several of the children could fit in at once.

But Asher, with the guidance of Mark, had draped their sheets and blankets over the couch and stuck two plastic children's chairs on the coffee table to form the largest fort by far.

"Think this is big enough for all of you to watch a movie in?" One of Mark's eyebrows went up.

The children all cheered and laughed and begged him to let them do it. It took a while to decide on a movie that was suitable for all of them, but finally Mark set up the family laptop inside the biggest fort, got the movie queued, handed the kids some popcorn, and let them watch.

Taking her hand, he steered her toward the kitchen. "We now have about ninety minutes to ourselves. Any ideas what you want to do?"

Kristan pulled out the biggest pout she could. "You mean we can't watch the movie in the blanket fort, too?"

His mouth twisted to the side. "If that's what you want to do. Or we could go inside one of the others and have some grown-up time." His eyebrows wiggled up and down.

"As much as that sounds nice, maybe not with the children right here."

"Spoilsport."

She attempted a seductive look. "How about I give you a rain check?"

Mark froze in place and narrowed his eyes. "I'd like that. For now, how about a game of rummy. You used to be pretty fierce if I recall."

"I'm still fierce."

Mark dug out a pack of cards, and they sat at the kitchen table. Over the next ninety minutes, they played cards, had a few snacks, and chatted about some of their old friends who Mark hadn't seen yet.

"Did you know Erik Storm came back from overseas pretty banged up and scarred? It was a bombing, I heard."

"Edele mentioned something about that. And he got married and adopted a few kids?"

"Yeah, he and Tessa spent their wedding night at The Inn. She's very sweet, though awfully quiet. They have another one now, too. A baby boy, I believe. They'll be at the anniversary party for his grandparents, Hans and Ingrid, tomorrow night. I've been working hard to make sure it's perfect. They deserve a beautiful night."

Mark reached over and patted her hand. "If you've got anything to do with it, I'm sure it will be everything they want it to be."

Kristan leaned in closer at the same time Mark tugged on her hand. His eyes were telling her things she'd wanted to hear for ten years. Just another inch and their lips would—

"The movie's over," AJ shouted. "Can we watch another one?"

Kristan sprang back and sucked in a gulp of air. Mark seemed to be breathing heavier, too, but he shook off the desire that had blanketed them and stood.

"Nope. Movie time is over, and bedtime has begun. First, though, we need to deconstruct the forts."

Whines and moans echoed from the blankets on the couch.

"But they're so cool." Kristan couldn't tell which of the boys had said that, but it was followed by agreement from the rest.

"I'll take some pictures so we can show your folks, but I'm pretty sure your mom won't be thrilled to come back to this."

The kids trooped out of the fort.

They took their time removing the sheets and blankets and getting in pajamas. Kristan said good night to the children, then Mark marched them upstairs. It was fifteen minutes before he came down again.

"Sorry about that. Aeryn wanted a story, and the older boys needed some serious man time to discuss things they couldn't talk to their dad about."

"What? They're eight and ten. Don't tell me they're interested in girls already."

"You told me you thought I was cute when you were ten."

Kristen laughed. "Yeah, but girls are far more advanced than boys."

Mark's eyes gleamed. "True. The boys only wanted to talk about a kid at school who used some bad words. They didn't want to say them in front of their dad."

"You had some cool uncle advice, I'm sure."

"Of course, because I'm the cool uncle. Now, I need to be the cool brother and wash these sheets. I'm sure Edele won't be happy seeing all her nice clean sheets wadded up in a ball."

They spent some time washing the sheets, folding the blankets, and generally tidying up the downstairs rooms. Kristan was surprised at how neat and organized Mark was.

"Ten years in the navy taught me a lot. The quarters we had were so tight you couldn't have anything be messy."

Once the sheets were in the dryer, Mark led her into the family room and clicked on the TV. It was like old times, sitting near each other on the couch watching a movie. But like old times, she didn't let herself get too close to him. In the past, it was because they were afraid their parents would object if they were caught.

Now, Kristan was more afraid of what getting close to Mark could do to her if he didn't stick around.

CHAPTER NINE

Footsteps echoed behind her, but Kristan knew it was Mark even before she turned around. She could smell that unique scent that was exclusively his. He'd never been one for heavy cologne or aftershave. He'd never needed it, either.

"Hey, Mark. What are you doing in my neck of the woods?" Otherwise known as her function hall.

That adorable grin nearly knocked her off her feet. After seeing how good he was with his niece and nephews last night, she had fallen even harder for him. There was absolutely no denying it. How would she ever bounce back when he left this time?

Because he would leave. After seeing the world and traveling all over, would he truly want to stay here in little Squamscott Falls, New Hampshire? Doubtful. Maybe if she were lucky, he would choose somewhere kind of close like Boston. It was only an hour's drive.

"You said you had the big Storm anniversary party tonight. I thought I'd see if you needed anyone to sweep a broom or move tables and chairs."

"I was just about to start the floors. You know where the broom is if you really want to help. You don't have to."

Mark shrugged as he headed toward the closet. "I like the company."

Heat rushed over her cheeks, and Kristan was glad he wasn't facing her now to see it.

Like the last time, Mark handled the broom and mop efficiently and had the tables and chairs in place quicker than she and the two waitresses she'd hired to come in early.

"Is Sofie Storm doing the decorations again or do you have everything here?" Mark pushed in the last chair at the table he'd just added a tablecloth to.

"She's using some of the Christmas decorations we had for the holiday parties earlier this week. Saves money and finding a place to store the stuff."

"So, what's next, boss?"

Kristan rolled her eyes at the name and was about to look at her list when a cry came from the kitchen, and Dottie, the assistant to the chef, came running out. "Sebastian just cut his hand. It's bleeding all over the place."

Kristan took off running and skidded to a stop at the sight of their chef holding a white towel around his hand. The towel was quickly turning red. Mark took the man's hand and gently folded the fabric away.

"That's going to need stitches. It looks fairly deep."

Oh, no. This was not what she needed on the day of a big party for a prominent local family. Not that the Storms wouldn't understand if the food wasn't ready. They were the nicest family she knew. But they were expecting over a hundred guests.

Mark gazed her way. "Do you have someone who can take him to the hospital?"

Dottie stepped near. "I can do it."

Panic punched her in the stomach. "No, I need you here to prep the food."

Dottie's face reflected Kristan's insides. "I can't do all this by myself. I'm not a chef, I just do what the chef tells me to."

Mark cleared his throat. "We'll figure something out. Right now, we need a driver. Krissy, can one of the staff do it?"

Nodding, she pointed at Dottie and instructed, "Get Gary. He should be in the storage room digging out the Christmas decorations."

Dottie took off while Mark wrapped another dishtowel around Sebastian's hand.

The chef was shaking his head and sweating. "I don't know how I did this. Stupid, stupid. The knife somehow slipped, I guess."

Kristan had a feeling Sebastian had been distracted by his helper. Even though Dottie was close to forty, she was a cute little thing with a stunning figure, and the chef had a roaming eye.

"It doesn't matter. All that's important is to get it fixed up."

Gary appeared in the door, and between her and Mark, they got Sebastian in the car and on his way. As they trudged back into the building, she leaned against the door and sighed. What the heck was she supposed to do now?

"I don't suppose he'll be able to come back and finish the meal prep."

Mark pulled her into his arms and held her tight. Yes, she needed this right now. She was supposed to handle every problem that came along, but this was unexpected. The chef they used when Sebastian was off was away visiting family this week. Mark's arms made her forget her dilemma for a few moments.

"Don't worry about anything, Krissy. I can help out."

Gazing into his eyes, she tried to believe it. "I know you've been so amazing with set up and everything, but I've got a hundred people to feed tonight."

"Is it a plated dinner?"

"No, we rarely do that. It's a buffet and self-serve. But the food still needs to be cooked and ready on time."

"Then, that's easy enough as long as you've got the menu and ingredients."

"This isn't a backyard barbecue, Mark."

"I know it isn't." He pressed a kiss to the tip of her nose. "I did a good deal of the meal prep on board the ship. We had a few hundred hungry sailors to feed. I told you I was good in the kitchen. Let's go take a look."

In the kitchen, Dottie had a mop out and was cleaning up the blood that had spilled. Kristan led Mark to the clipboard with tonight's menu. He studied it for a bit, then nodded.

"Totally doable. Show me where the food is kept and what you use for keeping it warm."

"You can really do this?"

At his nod, she wrapped her arms around his neck and squeezed. Mark's hand found her back and rubbed up and down.

"I'm sure with Dottie's help, we can get everything done in time. Hopefully as good as Chef's."

Kristan took a few minutes for a tour of the kitchen and food storage. "Dottie can show you where the utensils and pots and pans are and anything else if you can't find it. Right?"

Dottie perked up and grinned. "Absolutely. That's what I'm here for…to help."

The look in the woman's eyes as she stared at Mark said she'd be willing to do a lot more for him. Maybe Kristan should…no, she didn't have time for that now. Mark was already pulling out pans and bowls and putting ingredients on the large prep center. His attention was on the menu, not his assistant.

"Okay, if you need me, I'll be out in the function room. The party starts at six with hors d'oeuvres, and the meal should be ready to go by seven. I know that's hours away, but Sebastian usually prepped everything ahead of time, so it was ready to come out of the oven right on time."

Mark glanced up from the recipe book. "I'm good, Krissy. Go do what you need to do. Don't worry about the food. It's all taken care of."

She peeked back over her shoulder one last time, but Mark had gone back to prepping, giving Dottie instructions on what he needed from the freezer. Yup, she'd still worry, but Mark seemed at ease with what he was doing. She'd have to trust him.

Entering the function room, she found Sofie, her sister, Leah, and their cousin, Amy, along with Gina, all placing the centerpieces on the tables. While she'd been dealing with the crisis, they'd turned the room into a Christmas wonderland. Snowflakes, ornaments, a few nutcrackers, angels, and an assortment of framed pictures of their grandparents during the years filled the room. Enough to make the room festive but not too overwhelming.

"The place looks great, Sofie. You brought a team this time, I see."

Sofia tucked her blonde hair behind her ears and smirked. "I would have brought my brother, but I've seen him decorate. Greg's idea of high concept is strategically placing empty beer bottles around the room."

"Good idea to leave him at home." Should she tell them about the change in chef? She'd peek in on Mark in a bit and make a decision then. For now, she still had items to check off her list.

~

Mark adjusted the last stuffed mushroom on the tray, then nodded at the waitress to bring the food to the function room. Making the appetizers and meal for the anniversary party had been extremely tiring, but if he was truthful, fun.

Dottie was an adequate assistant and knew where everything was, even if she wasn't so great with any of the cooking. But Mark loved to cook. Glancing around the kitchen, he peeked to make sure everything was on schedule. Kristan liked her schedules. The sailors on board his ship also had schedules to keep, so he'd learned to be efficient when he cooked.

The last batch of appetizers had just gone out, and the main meal was almost ready to put in the chafing dishes. Dottie had already gotten the pans of warm water onto the trolleys.

Kristan came rushing in, her face pink, though the rest of her was as put together as always. A cream-colored dress with red and green accents hugged her curves lovingly.

"Mark, you've saved the day. The appetizers have been excellent, and everyone has nothing but great things to say. How are you doing with the main course?"

Mark pointed to the pans waiting on the trolleys, then pointed to the ovens. "The vegetables will come out last as we want them nice and hot. I'm just about to take the sirloin tips out, so they can rest for a few moments, and the Chicken Marsala will be ready at the same time as the vegetables. The rice pilaf is cooked. Just needs to be put in a pan. Dottie already brought out the rolls, butter, and other condiments. They're on the banquet table."

Kristan's shoulders sagged in relief. Had she thought he couldn't do this? A huge smile brightened her face, and he almost drew her into his arms for a kiss. Except she was in business mode right now, and he knew well enough to not mix business with pleasure. Too bad. Kissing her sure gave him pleasure.

"Can I do anything to help?" She glanced around the kitchen.

"Sure. Can you scoop out the rice while I hold the pot? It's easier with two people." Dottie could have helped him, but he liked looking at Krissy more.

They worked together to get both meat dishes, the veggies, rice, and the creamy tomato soup onto the rolling trays and wheeled out, where they transferred them onto the banquet tables. Kristen then strolled to where Hans and Ingrid Storm, Mr. And Mrs. Storm to him, he'd never called them anything else, and spoke to them quietly.

The anniversary couple held hands and crossed the room to the food. Mark stood nervously behind the tables.

"If there's anything else you need, let me know."

Hans smiled but gazed at his wife of sixty-five years and shook his head. "She's the only thing I've ever needed."

The words hit Mark right in the gut. He wanted that kind of love and longevity. There was only one woman who would ever make him feel the way Hans felt for Ingrid.

Ingrid laughed, her smile as large and loving as her husband's.

The rest of the family lined up and trooped past the food, scooping from each dish. Mark ran back and made sure the second round of food was ready to bring out as soon as the first had run out. For the next half hour, he hustled back and forth between the kitchen and the function hall, making sure everyone had enough. By the time the last guest strolled past the banquet tables, Mark breathed a sigh that he'd made enough. There was still some left in each dish.

Kristan made her way back to him after wandering through the room during the meal. When they were sure all had been adequately fed, he and Dottie whisked the trays away to the kitchen, where they bagged the rest of the food to be taken home by staff or left in the fridge for the staff to snack on the next few days.

He started to wash some of the pans, but Dottie stopped him. "That's my job. You did all the food prep. Go relax for a bit. Sebastian never did much beyond the cooking."

Mark wanted to object, but Krissy slid her hand around his elbow and tugged him to stand in the doorway of the function room. The waitresses were starting to clean up plates of those who had already finished.

"Should we...?" He pointed to the room.

"No, that's what I hire waitstaff for. They'll clean the tables, and once the happy couple have done the initial cut for the cake, they'll cut the rest so the guests can enjoy. They're also responsible for doing the dishes and putting everything away. They like the extra pay they get for the extra hours."

"You've got this down pretty much to a science, huh?"

"I try. I'm sure there are some areas that could use some work, but I haven't been manager here all that long."

Mark could think of a few things in the kitchen that could use streamlining. He'd never want to step on the chef's toes, but maybe he'd mention a few to Kristan before he left.

The Storm family and all their friends milled around the room, chatting and enjoying themselves. At one point, Luke strolled past with his mother, Molly, and his aunt, Luci. They stopped right in front of Kristan.

"The food was very good, Kristan. As always," Luke said.

"Actually." Molly tilted her head and pursed her lips. "I'd say it was even better than at Sara's wedding. Not that hers wasn't excellent. What did Sebastien do differently?"

Krissy straightened up and smoothed down her skirt. "Sebastian had a little accident this afternoon unfortunately.

Nothing major, some stitches in his hand. Luckily, we had a last-minute stand in. You know Mark Campbell, right?"

She turned slightly to indicate him. They all greeted him.

Luci hummed and winked. "Outstanding, I'd say. You might want to keep him on, Kristan."

The Storms drifted away, and Kristan faced him. "What did you do differently? I didn't get a chance to taste any of the food."

"Nothing major. I just added a little something here and subtracted a bit of something there. Sorry if I shouldn't have, but I'm used to cooking to taste, not to a recipe."

Krissy's eyes went wide. "Are you kidding me? Luci Storm says it was outstanding, then the food was outstanding. Maybe you'll have to give Sebastian a few pointers."

Mark wasn't sure that would go over too well. Most chefs weren't open to changing their recipes.

"Speaking of which." Krissy bit her bottom lip. She only did that when she was nervous about something, which was rare for the highly organized woman. "He sent me a text about an hour ago. Seems he won't be able to use his hand for two weeks. Not if he wants it to heal correctly."

"Geesh. I'm sorry. Let me know if there's anything I can do."

Her shoulders rose, and a sly look crossed her face. "If you're offering…we have a very important event New Year's Eve. A big party sponsored by the local Chamber of Commerce for all the area small businesses. They do this every year, and the last three years they've chosen our inn to hold it. It's a huge honor."

"And you need a chef. What's the schedule of service for that one?"

"Appetizers from eight to nine, then the buffet needs to be available from nine to ten-thirty. Similar foods to tonight with a few more choices. I want to have snacks like crackers, cheese, and fruit out for the rest of the night, since the bar will be open, and we don't need empty bellies with lots of alcohol in them."

"Good thought." His gaze skimmed the room where the anniversary couple danced, holding each other close. "Will there be dancing?"

Kristan tipped her head, her brows knitting together. "Yes, there'll be a DJ."

"Okay, I'll do it. For a price."

"Of course, we'll pay you. I wouldn't expect you to do this for free." Her scowl was softened by her vulnerability.

Taking her hands, he brought them to his lips. "My price, dear lady, will be a dance with The Inn proprietress at the stroke of midnight."

"A dance? The proprietress could possibly be persuaded to have a dance with you."

Mark leaned back against the wall and tugged on Krissy's hand to stay close. The party was in full swing, everyone enjoying themselves.

Even using a cane to walk, his old buddy, Erik Storm, still looked healthy and strong playing with his two adopted children. Mark felt a tug of envy slice through him at how Erik stared at his wife. The man was enamored, no doubt, and his wife's shy smile as she held an infant to her shoulder mirrored his feelings right back.

Any jealousy he had for Alex Storm was swiftly swept away at how the man held his beloved when they danced. Alex had never been one for any kind of public display, but it was apparent to anyone with eyes that he loved Gina with all his heart.

The strange couple that was Nathaniel Storm and his intended, Darcy, still couldn't be faulted. The two young children he'd met after skating appeared happy while skipping around with a young man who looked just like Darcy.

When he asked Kristan, she told him it was Darcy's brother, Zane. Extended family and all accepted as belonging here.

Sara Storm was held in the arms of a tall, dark, and handsome man, as they swayed to the music. Luke and Kevin Storm stood by the bar chatting with several young ladies, though he knew none of them were Storms.

His hockey buddy, Greg, chatted with his parents and sisters, while his son cavorted with some of the other children. If you didn't know the players, it would be difficult to put the smaller family groups together. Cousins, aunts, uncles, grandparents, all intermingled and took turns helping and having fun.

And the happy couple constantly gazed around at the beautiful family they had created with loving eyes. Could he have this someday? This huge loving family all enjoying themselves.

He glanced down at Krissy and squeezed her hand.

"Don't forget my payment for New Year's Eve."

After skimming the room, she faced him and her eyes twinkled. "A dance? We might be able to afford a little more than that."

Was she talking about the same thing he had on his mind? Hopefully. The longer he was in her presence, the more he wanted what the Storm family had.

CHAPTER TEN

The bell above the door tinkled as Kristan stepped inside Sweet Dreams. The smell of cinnamon and vanilla wafted her way, and her stomach rumbled. She could have snitched some of the pastry at The Inn, but on Sundays, Kelsey made Elephant Ears only for the store and Kristan couldn't resist.

As she got in the short line, she dug through her purse for her wallet. Laughter by the window brought her head up and eyes in that direction. Three men sat in one of the bistro sets, nursing coffees and a plate of homemade donuts. Even though his back was to her, she knew the center one was Mark. Flanking him were his old hockey teammates, Greg and Logan.

It seemed like they were catching up and having fun, so she didn't want to intrude. She'd make it a point to say hi on her way out. Maybe Mark would ask what she was doing today, and they could spend some time together. It was her day off, and she was only going to The Inn to check on a few things first.

As she moved up in line, she couldn't help but overhear

their conversation. Mark was describing in great detail some of the places he'd visited while in the navy.

"You wouldn't believe how beautiful the buildings are there. This big, huge city bustling with people, and it's been there for thousands of years. Incredible."

"What are some places you wished you'd gone but didn't get a chance to see?" Greg asked.

"When I was in the Mediterranean, Greece was so gorgeous, but there were a few islands I missed and can't wait to go back to. Put it on that old bucket list."

The person in front of her stepped away from the counter, and Kristan faced Kelsey.

"Hey there. I put aside an Elephant Ear just for you. Your regular coffee to go with it?"

Nodding, she said, "Thanks, Kels." Was her life so routine that she didn't even have to order?

The laughter from the nearby table had her mind racing in too many directions and over too many memories. Mark spending time with her here. Mark wanting to travel and see more of the world than he already had. The day he told her he was leaving. The pain of seeing him go and having no say in the matter. The lonely years without him. The recent days with him.

She handed Kelsey a ten and took the bag and cup, telling her to keep the change. She couldn't listen to Mark and his buddies any longer.

When she pushed open the door, his head jerked up and he called out, "Krissy, wait up."

Yelling a goodbye to his friends, Mark followed her out the door. It had been what she'd hoped for, but now she wasn't so sure.

She plastered on her best smile and said, "Thanks for helping out yesterday. We couldn't have done it without you. I appreciate your stepping up to the plate."

He quickened his pace to match hers. "You know I was happy to do it."

"I should draw something up for you with your pay rate for the New Year's party. Make it official."

Mark looked at her strangely, but she kept walking, taking tiny sips of her coffee. She'd enjoy her pastry when she got into her office. By herself.

"You know my price for being your temporary chef." His voice hummed with teasing. She took a deep breath and pushed away the longing that sprang up with the tone.

The town green—silly name since it was now covered in snow—was empty this morning. Skaters would drop by later in the day, but for now the gazebo glistened alone and the wind rustled through the evergreens causing the decorations to clink together.

When they got adjacent to The Inn, Kristan stopped and studied Mark.

"Did you ever regret leaving?" She had to know, despite not being sure what she wanted for an answer.

Mark let out a breath, the air turning into a white puff as it floated away. Placing his hands on her shoulders, he tilted forward. "I did. Every morning when I woke from my dreams of you and you weren't in my arms."

"You dreamed of me?" Was this all smoke and mirrors to get more time with her during his few days left? Or did he mean it?

"I dreamed of you so often, Krissy. Holding you. Kissing you."

Maybe that's all she was to him. Forgotten dreams.

"You know I had dreams of you, too. Mine weren't always as nice as what you had. It was me, standing outside, watching you leave, calling your name. Crying for you to come back. Begging you to bring my heart back to me. You stole it, you know. Took it with you wherever the heck you went. Not that I ever knew where it was. I could never fall for another guy because I didn't have anything to give him. You did that to me, Mark."

"God, Krissy, I'm so sorry. It wasn't my intention to hurt you."

Pulling away from his hands, she pressed her lips together to keep from crying. "But you did."

"I had to leave. Don't you see? You were so young and still needed to get through college. I couldn't even think about making a lifelong commitment to you at that point. I had things I needed to do, to see."

"It's nice that you could forget all about me. I never forgot about you. Never." A few tears trickled down her face, and she quickly swiped them away.

"You were always with me, Krissy. Everywhere I went." He dug his wallet out of this pocket and flipped it open. "See? You were right here."

It was a picture of them from her prom. The night they'd finally expressed their love for each other. But he must have known what he was planning then. Joining the navy. He'd signed up and shipped out two months later. Even knowing that he was leaving, he'd accepted the innocence she gave him. What a fool she'd been.

Was she being one now? He'd talked about staying and possibly finding a job nearby. *Possibly.* Getting to know her again. Then, what happened when he got tired of small-town living? Or had the desire to go see those unexplored villages in Greece? It might be months from now or even years. But the longer he stayed, the deeper her love for him grew. She'd never stopped loving him and probably never would. When he left, how would she ever put the shattered pieces of her heart back together again? She hadn't been able to in the last ten years. It would be an impossible task if she didn't stop this now.

"Mark, maybe we need to rethink this thing between us."

"Krissy, no. I know I've hurt you, but we're good together. You and me."

"I used to think that, too. And I do care about you so much." She couldn't admit she was still in love with him. He'd use it to his advantage. Of course, he'd left before without any kind of discussion with her. He could do it again.

She loved working at The Inn, even when it was a struggle running it solo. She'd learned so much about herself during that time. One of the biggest things was that she wanted to be equal to any partner she had. In all decision making. Mark had proved he didn't see her as an equal.

Shaking her head, she made a decision. "You broke my heart. I can't let you do it again."

KRISTAN PERUSED the crowded function hall and smiled. All was going well. The Chamber of Commerce had paid them a hefty fee to hold their party here. Additionally, all the small business owners got a chance to see what The Inn could do. A number of them had already mentioned to her about holding monthly meetings in their space. The function hall wasn't just for large parties and weddings. They had the capability to close off parts of the room to create smaller spaces. This made them more versatile and hopefully would get them more weekday business.

The waitresses had cleaned up the banquet table and were now cruising the room, picking up empty glasses and bottles people had discarded. So many guests had commented on the quality of the food, and she'd been graciously thanking them. Mark was the one to thank. He'd saved The Inn from a horrible fate.

Not that she'd thanked him today. She hadn't spoken with

him since she'd walked away from him Sunday morning. She'd made Macy or Dottie the go-between to ensure he had whatever he needed for the menu. Yes, she might have peeked in the kitchen just to convince herself he had everything under control, and she wasn't needed in there. She wasn't.

So many familiar faces in this room. People she worked with, like the linen service who washed all her tablecloths and napkins. The printer who created any signs and promotion they needed. The organic grocery store who got them locally grown food at wholesale prices.

Her friend, Kelsey, was here as the owner of Sweet Dreams, as was Logan representing the Granite Grill, and Kris, Nick, and Pete Storm for Storm Electric. John Michaels, who had a small renovation business, and Sofie Storm, who had started her own interior design company, were on the dance floor *cutting a rug*, as her grandmother used to call it. Even Alex, who owned his own local architecture firm, was grooving to the music with Gina. It was good to see people happy and enjoying themselves.

Standing off to the side, she tried to stay in the background. Shirley Irskine, the councilwoman who'd suggested The Inn for the party made sure to let her know she ran a business, too, and should enjoy herself. Kristan felt uncomfortable doing that while an event was going on. She needed to stay strictly in her professional demeanor.

As she snitched a cracker from one of the tables and popped it in her mouth, her phone vibrated in her pocket. Drawing it out, she took a peek at what had gone off. It was a response to the advertisement for a cook she'd put online. Even though Sebastian only needed two weeks for his hand to heal, she'd gotten vibes from him for a while that he wanted a full-time gig. It wasn't something The Inn could offer right now.

Clicking on the app, she scrolled through to bring up the application. Candidate's name: Mark Campbell. What? Mark had applied for the position?

She started reading through his resume and the answers to the questions she'd posted. His college degree was in business. He'd gone on to get an MBA, as well. While he was in the navy? Yeah, she'd heard they would pay for schooling. So why had he put in for a part-time chef position? It didn't make sense.

"Whatever you're reading seems riveting." Mark's deep voice startled her, and she dropped her phone. He scooped it mid-air and handed it back to her.

"What are you up to?" She held up the phone.

His shrug was casual. "I don't know what you're talking about. The meal is done, and I'm not needed for the snacks anymore."

"You applied for the chef position here. You don't have a background or training in being a chef."

He cocked his head and gazed up. "You're right. I don't have any *formal* training. But cooking for a few hundred or more people onboard a ship has to count for something. Besides, between tonight and the Storms' party, I proved I could be counted on to produce quality meals for a large group of people. Wouldn't you agree?"

No way she could dispute that. The guests had raved about the meal tonight and the variety of dishes available. Mark had doctored the menu tonight like he'd done on Saturday, and the result was outstanding. She'd made sure to sample everything that came out of the kitchen tonight.

"Why are you doing this, Mark? For me?"

A sheepish look crossed his face. "It's actually a bit more selfish than that. I want to be with you, Krissy. I've seen the world, and now I know that where I belong is here."

Could she believe him? "You'll be happy in this small town?"

"I'll be happy anywhere you are. You said I took your heart with me when I left, but mine stayed here with you. I missed you and thought of you every day. You were never far from my thoughts."

"You could have fooled me." Her pleasant demeanor had been pushed aside for the hurt and pain to surface.

"I know I didn't stay in touch like I should have. Like I promised you I would. And I regret that more than anything else. Even when I was trying to forget you, thinking you were getting on with your life with someone new, my heart never stopped loving you. I still love you, Krissy. I always will, regardless of what happens between us. Now I know I want to be with you. Here or anywhere. My home is with you."

Kristan slipped her phone in her pocket, giving her time to think. She had to focus on the application first. "Do you really want this job? Or is it just to be near me? Because I need someone who'll do the work and not take off when it's not exciting enough. I'd be your boss. Could you take orders from me? Or would you make decisions without my input like you've done in the past?"

"You run The Inn. I have a few ideas on how to streamline some of the food service to make everything run smoother, and I'd love to add some different choices to the menu, but the final decision for everything is all on you. Unless you wanted my help with anything else."

"Like what?" What was he getting at?

"I've got a degree in business and management. You've been telling me how difficult it's been doing this job by yourself. I've seen how many hours you put in. The Inn shows all your hard work. But if someone were around to give you a hand every now and then, would you accept it?"

She planted one hand on her hip. "You'd want to do the reception desk? Tidy up the breakfast room? Occasionally clean a room if the housekeeping staff is swamped?"

"I'd do anything that was needed. Like pushing a broom and moving tables. I haven't been too high and mighty the past two weeks to help out with those things."

He certainly had jumped in and made the work go faster and smoother. "You won't want to see more of the world? Like those Greek Islands you didn't get a chance to visit?"

His eyes narrowed, then his mouth opened in a grin. "Of course, I'd like to see them and so many other places, but I was hoping maybe I'd have someone to go with me."

"Are you looking at me? Because I have a business to run."

Mark set his hands on her shoulders and lowered his head. "Yes, you do. However, part of being a good business owner is knowing when you need to take a small break and let others do the work. Your dad might be thinking about retiring and travel, but he's still capable of keeping the inn running for a week or so. You know, so you can take a vacation every now and then. One or two weeks when The Inn has a slow time can be arranged."

What Mark said made sense. For the job. What about her?

"You won't get bored here?"

He stroked his fingers down her cheek. "Krissy, I enjoyed working here for these two events and seeing what you did on Christmas Day. It looks like there's a new challenge every day. How could I get bored? But if you don't want me working here, or don't think we could work together while being in a relationship, that's fine, too. I'll find another job nearby. I'm not going anywhere, Krissy. I made a mistake once by not including you in my decisions, I won't do that again."

"I need someone who'll do a great job with this, and I

know you will. But I also need…" How did she put this into words?

Mark kissed the tip of her nose. "I don't want to lose you again. I love you and need you in my life."

His eyes shone with that deep emotion and her heart thudded loudly in her chest, begging her to take another chance. "You need me in your life? For how long?"

"I want everything with you, Krissy. The house, the white picket fence, a passel of kids, and maybe even a dog. An Irish Setter would be great, but that can be negotiated."

"I love you, too, Mark. I've been so afraid of getting hurt again, I've pushed you away."

"And I deserved it. But I need you in my life. I'm not going anywhere without you and will stick around until I've shown you that I'm serious. You're the only woman for me, and I plan on spending every day for the rest of my life proving that to you."

Excitement danced in her veins. "Every day, huh?"

He cupped her face lovingly in his hands and pressed the most beautiful kiss to her lips.

"Every single day. Forever, if you'll have me."

Kristan smiled as the clock struck midnight, ringing in the new year. She pulled his head down, not caring that their love was on display for all to see. She was in Mark's arms, finally where she belonged.

"Forever. That's the only way I'll take you."

~

Take a sneak peek at where the Storms began. ELUSIVE DREAMS Book 1 Storms of New England.

ELUSIVE DREAMS

STORMS OF NEW ENGLAND, BOOK 1

CHAPTER ONE

'*Save my babies, please.*'

The words echoed through Captain Erik Storm's head like an 80 mm mortar attack. Reaching for the crutches, he slid out of the minivan. The images of the bombed-out cellar, where he'd spent four days of misery, flashed through his mind like sniper fire.

Fuckin' hell. What had he been thinking? No way he was in any shape to take care of two young children. It didn't matter if they were arriving in four days or four months. He couldn't even walk on his own. And who the hell knew if he ever would. The doctors hadn't even been sure.

But he'd promised. Sure, only to reassure Matteen and Kinah's dying mom that they'd have a good life in the States versus whatever hell awaited them in a Kandahar orphanage. And with their grandfather having been British, their chances of surviving until adulthood were slim. He'd gotten to know them during the ordeal. Their silly games, their precious smiles, even their inability to stay quiet when he needed them to. When the mortar fire had exploded above them, he'd kept them occupied. Sacrificed his water and

MREs to keep them somewhat hydrated and nourished. Held and rocked them when they were tired but too scared to sleep. Then comforted them when their mother had finally succumbed to her injuries.

He slammed the car door, which gave him only a momentary satisfaction, then shifted the crutches under his arms and hobbled to the back of the vehicle. Somehow he needed to get the food into the house. There was no grocery cart here to wheel it along.

The salty scent of coastal Maine assaulted his nostrils as he opened the back of the van. He'd loved coming here as a kid. His grandparents had decided not to sell the place after they'd moved back to New Hampshire and for that he was grateful. It was perfect for what he needed to do. The next step in his life.

But now he needed to get everything inside. The groceries he could bring in a few bags at a time but what about the other supplies? Like the baby crib and high chair? Maybe he should have taken his brothers up on their offer to help. But no, he had to be a stubborn Marine and show he could do everything himself. Maybe he could leave the heavy stuff in there for a few days, eat some crow and call Alex and Luke. They'd bust his balls but what did that matter, it wasn't like he'd be using them anymore. His bashed in leg and hip had resulted in other damage. Stuff you couldn't see.

He gritted his teeth and pushed those thoughts back in the furthest part of his mind then reached in for the grocery bags. His left crutch slipped as he grabbed a second bag and he swore again as he bumped into the side of the van. Even after a month, the friggin' wounds were still tender. Maybe he could use just one crutch. The shattered knee and fractured pelvis were both on the left side. Switching the right crutch to his left arm, he slid his right hand through the handles of several plastic bags. See, manageable.

Until he took a few steps. At the pressure, pain sliced through his left leg and he stumbled, dropping the bag the eggs were in.

"Shit, damn, fuck."

As he bent to pick up the bag, the brace holding his knee in place was too bulky and threw him off balance, tossing him on the ground. The driveway met his ass sending his hip into spasms. Heat surged through him along with the pain and he flung the crutch at the car. It smacked into the bumper and fell with a thud, a good five feet out of his reach.

"Nice going, dickhead. Now you need to crawl across the ground to get it."

Maybe he could sit here and wait for his knee and hip to heal enough so he could actually move. Right, 'cause that was sensible. At this moment he didn't feel like doing sensible. He felt like punching something. Hard.

He took a few deep breaths and called on the control the Corp was so famous for. Before he could start the familiar army crawl a soft voice floated over.

"Do you need some help?"

"Shit, damn, fuck."

The words drifted over to Tessa Porter as she opened the door to let her cat, Calico, into the house. Her gaze moved to the Storm's house next door where a light blue minivan sat in the driveway. It didn't belong to Hans or Ingrid, but they had three sons and ten grandkids. It could be any one of theirs.

More grumbled swears made their way over and she took a few tentative steps down from her porch. Did someone need help? It wasn't obvious from her position so she walked closer waiting to check what the situation was. The Storms were all nice, but she wasn't the type to barge in where she wasn't needed.

A crutch bounced off the back fender startling her. A crutch? Did the person swearing need it? Probably, if the cursing was anything to go by. She moved around the end of the vehicle and there, on the ground, sat Erik Storm, his face a mixture of pain and frustration.

Erik. Why did it have to be Erik? Of all the Storm cousins, he was the one she'd had the biggest crush on. And most likely he knew it. She'd avoided him like the plague and had barely been able to string two words together when he was near.

"Do you need some help?"

Stupid question. The huge brace on his knee, poking out from his cargo shorts, attested to some sort of injury and the crutch only confirmed that. Actually there was another crutch sticking out from under the other side of the van. Had he been injured in the war? His grandparents had told her he was oversees. Obviously not anymore.

He gazed up at her, his expression thunderous. She took a step back. Maybe she should turn around and go home. Run home. Fast. He didn't look like he was in a good mood.

"Tessa." Her name came out softer than she would have imagined with the scowl still on his face. "I'm fine. Thanks."

Giving a quick nod, she backed away, but he swore under his breath and called her again.

"Tessa, sorry. No, I'm not okay. But I'm being stubborn. If I can swallow my pride for a minute, maybe you can give me a hand."

"Sure." Had she been loud enough to hear? She moved forward again but slowly.

A smile, a real one this time formed on his lips. He held up his hand. "Could you get the crutches? Please."

The last word was like an afterthought. But Hans and

Ingrid had hammered manners into all their grandkids. There was no way he could be rude.

Picking up the crutch closest to her, she handed it to him then retrieved the other one. He struggled for a minute, folding his good leg under him, and attempted to push himself up with a crutch in each hand.

"Do you want help?" Why had she opened her mouth and asked? He'd probably just scowl at her again. Touching him wasn't in her plans either. Not good for her nerves.

He clenched his teeth and faked a smile. "If you don't mind."

She moved up behind him, put her hands under his arms, and lifted. The muscles hidden by his T-shirt strained as he pushed on the crutches but soon he was standing. For a moment he balanced then took a deep breath in. As soon as he seemed stable, she let go. Those few seconds had been far too long for her.

"Thanks. I'm not usually so clumsy but well…" He glanced at the metal and fabric wrapped around his leg. *Look away from the muscular calves or you'll be stammering like the idiot you usually are.*

"No problem. Do you want help getting the groceries inside?"

Throwing her a wry grin, he nodded. "Sure, I've got no pride left anymore. What the hell."

"Is the door unlocked?"

He shook his head. "I just got here. Stopped at the store first. Didn't figure I'd have any problems. Dumb ass." The last words were muttered under his breath and she pinched her lips together to keep from smiling. This self-deprecating Erik was kind of adorable.

When he grinned again, heat rose to her cheeks. God, why couldn't she be normal around him? Around any guy? It had been over ten years. She wanted to be normal.

"Why don't you unlock the door and I'll bring in the bags." There weren't too many, and she could loop the handles around her hands and carry more of them.

He sighed, maneuvering his way up the few porch steps and into the house. Once she grabbed some bags, she followed him. Already he was setting a few bags on the counter. She walked through the large family room with the gorgeous ocean views and entered the airy kitchen.

She'd always loved this house. The windows on the ocean side were large and unobstructed and it felt like you were practically standing in the waves. Usually the breeze blew through and you could smell the salt air. Not today. The house had been closed up for a few weeks at least. That was the last time Hans and Ingrid had been here.

"Your grandparents were up a short while ago but didn't say anything about your coming here." She dropped the bags on the kitchen table.

"They didn't know. I only got back home last week."

"There're a few bags left. I'll get them while you put the food away." Erik wouldn't want to look like he couldn't handle a task so she'd given him something to do. His crooked smile told her he appreciated it.

When she came back in, he was studying the contents of the egg carton. He held it up and smirked. "Want an omelet? A few of these are cracked, but I think I can still use them."

"Thank you but I'm—"

"It's the least I can do. Give me a little of my masculinity back by accepting my offer. I make a mean omelet."

"I know you do. I've had them at The Boat House." Years ago when she bussed tables and he cooked. And she'd dropped silverware every time he'd looked at her. God, how embarrassing.

"That's right," he chuckled. "You used to take any of the extra parts that didn't fit on the plate when I had an order."

Should she stay and let him make her an omelet? That meant she'd have to talk to him. It wasn't something she did all that well and especially not with Erik Storm. But his eyes were begging her and she never could resist anything he asked of her. Luckily, he'd never asked too much.

"I don't want to put you out and eat all your eggs." One last chance to let him get out of it.

Erik limped to the counter and pulled out a bowl. "I need to use the broken ones now anyway. And there are..." He looked in the egg carton then back up. "Five of them. I like to eat but I think five eggs is a bit much even for me. You'd be doing me a favor. And letting me pay you back for getting me up a few minutes ago."

"Okay, but let me help." At his tired look she added, "I always wanted to learn your secret for perfect omelets."

His lips twisted, and one eyebrow rose. "The secret's in the way you cook it, not the ingredients. Can you grab the frying pan in that cabinet?"

He pointed to the one she was standing near and she bent over to retrieve it. Taking it from her he placed it on the stove. After cracking open the already fractured eggs, he started whisking them with a fork.

"Is ham and cheese okay for today? Onions and peppers will take too long to chop up."

She nodded. For today? Did that mean he'd make her some another day? Did she want to sit with him and have conversation more than once? Although maybe when he realized she sucked at small talk, he wouldn't ask again. That's what most people did. Her extreme introversion made most people uncomfortable.

"I'll get a few plates." She bustled around the kitchen so she wouldn't have to chat and he wouldn't need to find something to say. Although he'd always been outgoing. Conversations flowed freely around him. She sighed.

Wouldn't it be nice if she could be that way? After so many years of trying, she wasn't sure it would ever happen.

When dishes, napkins and silverware were on the table, she sat down and watched as Erik chopped the ham and finished creating his masterpiece. She took the opportunity to really study him. While he rested on his right leg, his left leg stayed slightly bent with the brace. What happened?

His blond military cut, she suspected, was a little longer than was traditional. When had he been injured? Wide shoulders filled out the T-shirt in ways she shouldn't be thinking about and then narrowed down to slim hips. She'd seen him before he was deployed, and he'd been much bulkier, more buff. Had he lost weight with his injury? Or being in a war zone? He still looked amazing to her though. Always had.

Her gaze moved to the scar on his face running from his hairline and crossing through his right eyebrow. When he turned to grab the spatula, she saw another, deeper one, starting on his jaw line and ending at his left ear. It should have taken away from his good looks, but it simply made him look more human. He'd always been far too perfect.

"Can you grab these plates so I don't end up with egg all over my face, literally?"

Bouncing up, she took the plates he held out and returned to the table so he could shuffle over on his crutches without an audience. Being seen as weak would be something he'd hate since he'd always been so athletic and in shape. And would be again when this injury healed.

"Let me know if cracked eggs work as well as whole ones. I'm kind of curious."

She bit into her omelet but couldn't help notice Erik glanced down at his leg when he'd mentioned the cracked eggs. Did he wonder if he was still as good as someone whole?

She closed her eyes at the taste of the eggs, ham, cheese,

and spices, all precisely blended together and cooked to perfection. Heaven. Just as she remembered.

"It's amazing, like you always made them."

"Thanks." The gratitude in his voice surprised her. He'd never been the timid type or in any way lacking self-esteem. Suddenly he was in need of praise?

She took her time eating the meal so she didn't have to come up with conversation. He didn't seem to mind the lull and paid attention to his own food. How long would he be here? A few days? A week or more? How could she avoid him if he was staying here? Their houses were fairly close and their driveways were side by side. And she worked out of the house so she was home every day. If at all possible, she steered clear of going out anywhere.

The weather this July had been beautiful and not too humid. Spending days outside and working with her computer from her back deck was typical. The thought of staying in all day so she didn't have to see him wasn't a pleasant one. And to get to the path leading to the ocean trail, she had to go past his house.

"So, how've you been?" He finally asked having eaten most of his omelet.

She swallowed what was in her mouth. *Don't let me have anything stuck to my teeth.* "Fine." Oh, great answer. Now ask him something back. But not how he's been since, duh, brace on his leg.

"How long are you staying here?" Lifting her fork, she finished her last bite. It was his turn to speak, she could risk it.

"Actually, I'm moving in. I'm buying the place from my grandparents and plan on living here year round."

The fork dropped from her hand and clattered on the table.

ABOUT THE AUTHOR

Purchase links to all retailers here:

https://www.karilemor.com/books

To get firsthand information and notices of sales and new releases, plus free stories and bonus scenes, sign up for Kari's newsletter here:

https://www.karilemor.com/

Join her reader's Group THE LIT LOUNGE for fun and getting to know her better:

https://www.facebook.com/groups/373521153021256/

Other places to get information on Kari:

- facebook.com/Karilemorauthor
- twitter.com/karilemor
- instagram.com/karilemorauthor
- pinterest.com/karilemor
- bookbub.com/authors/kari-lemor

Made in United States
North Haven, CT
19 July 2023